우리 문학은 우리 문화의 또 다른 창입니다. 한림출판사는 한국 현대 단편 문학의 숨은 보석과 같은 작품들을 엄선, '글'과 더불어 조화로운 이중주를 연주하기 위한 '그림' 작업을 더하여 세계의 관객을 향해 다가가고자 합니다. 우리의 '한글'과 더불어 세계인과 소통할 수 있는 '영어'와의 이중주를 통해 세계의 무대 위에 서서 우리의 이야기를 시작하고자 합니다. Literature often offers readers a special window into a country's culture. This is especially true in Korea's case, which is in part why Hollym is proud to be associated with this special project that provides readers with a collection of stories presented in both English and Korean, with accompanying illustrations, as it will help people from around the world better understand Korea's time-honored and unique culture. At the same time, it will expose a new generation of readers to many of Korea's most respected authors and short stories.

The Snowy Road 눈길

Hollym
Elizabeth, NJ · Seoul

눈길 The Snowy Road

1판 1쇄 발행_ 2004년 5월31일
1판 2쇄 발행_ 2005년 3월31일

지은이_ 이청준
옮긴이_ 이현재
그린이_ 최재은
꾸민곳_ 스튜디오 바프
　　　　프로듀서/크리에이티브 디렉터: 이나미
　　　　진행/디자인: 김선희, 이여형

펴낸이_ 함기만
펴낸곳_ 한림출판사
　　　　진행/편집: 이희정
등록_ 1963년 1월 18일(제1-443호)
주소_ 서울 종로구 관철동 13-13, 우편번호 110-111
전화_ (02)735-7551~4 팩스_ (02)730-5149
홈페이지_ http://www.hollym.co.kr 이메일_ info@hollym.co.kr

Text Copyright © 2004 by Yi Chong-jun
English Translation Copyright © 2004 by Hyun-jae Yee Sallee
Illustration Copyright © 2004 by Choi Jea eun
Production Copyright © 2004 by Studio BAF

English translation of "The Snowy Road" by Yi Chong-jun copyright © 1993
by Hyun-jae Yee Sallee from *The Snowy Road and Other Stories* (Buffalo, New York: White Pine Press) used by permission of the publisher.

All rights reserved. No part of this book may be reproduced in any form,
except for brief quotation for a review or in scholarly essays and books,
without the prior written permission of the publisher.

First published in 2004
Second printing, 2005
by Hollym International Corp.
18 Donald Place, Elizabeth, NJ 07208, USA
Phone: (908) 353-1655　　Fax: (908) 353-1655
http://www.hollym.com

Published simultaneously in Korea by Hollym Corporation; Publishers
13-13, Gwancheol-dong, Jongno-gu, Seoul 110-111, Korea
Phone: (02) 735-7551~4　　Fax: (02) 730-5149, 8192
http://www.hollym.co.kr　E-mail: info@hollym.co.kr

ISBN: 1-56591-203-9
Library of Congress Control Number: 2004103835

Printed in Korea

작가 이청준은 1939년 전라남도 장흥 출생으로 서울대학교 문리대 독어독문학과를 졸업하였다. 1965년에 〈사상계〉 신인상에 「퇴원」으로 당선되어 등단하였으며, 「병신과 머저리」로 동인문학상 (1968), 「잔인한 도시」로 이상문학상(1978), 「비화밀교」로 대한민국문학상(1986), 「자유의 문」으로 이산문학상(1990), 「날개의 집」으로 제1회 21세기문학상(1998)을 수상하였다. Yi Chong-jun was born in 1939 in Jangheung, South Jeolla Province. He studied German Language and Literature at Seoul National University. Since his debut in 1965 with the publication of *Toewon (Hospital Discharge)* in *Sasanggye* magazine, he has won numerous awards for his literary works, including the 1968 Dongin Literature Award for *Byeongsin-gwa meojeori (The Idiot and the Fool)*, the 1978 Yi Sang Literature Award for *Janinhan dosi (The Cruel City)*, the 1986 Republic of Korea Literature Award for *Bihwamilgyo (Esoteric Buddhism)*, the 1990 Isan Literature Award for *Jayu-ui mun (The Gate of Freedom)*, and the first 21st Century Literature Award for *Nalgae-ui jip (The House of Wings)* in 1998.

번역자 이현재는 한국문화예술진흥원이 후원하는 1989년 번역상 수상작가로 미국, 캐나다, 영국, 호주 그리고 한국에서 다수의 번역 작품을 발표했다. 대산문화재단(1995)과 한국문화예술진흥원(1999)의 번역지원금 수혜자이다. Hyun-jae Yee Sallee was the recipient of the 1989 Translation Award sponsored by the Korean Culture and Arts Foundation. Her translations have appeared in publications throughout the U.S.A., Canada, England, Australia, and Korea. Previous translations include: *A Sketch of the Fading Sun* (White Pine Press, 1999), a collection of short stories by Pak Wan-suh; *The Snowy Road* (White Pine Press, 1993); *Selected Poems of Kim Namjo* (Cornell University Press, 1993) co-translated with David R. McCann; and *The Waves* (Kegan Paul International, 1989). She received translation grants from the Daesan Foundation in 1955 and from KCAF in 1999.

일러스트레이터 최재은은 서울에서 태어나 자랐고 미국의 Pratt Institute와 School of Visual Arts 대학원에서 일러스트레이션을 전공하였다. 지금은 명지대학교에서 교수로 재직하며 일러스트레이터로 활동하고 있다. Society of Illustrators of LA 주최의 일러스트레이션 공모전에서 금상 수상을 비롯, Communication Arts, Graphis 등의 국제 일러스트레이션 공모전에서 10여 차례 수상한 바 있다. Choi Jae-eun studied Illustration at the Pratt Institute and received graduate training at the School of Visual Arts in New York. She is currently a professor at Myongji University and a prolific illustrator. She has received prizes at ten international illustration competitions, including Communication Arts, Graphis, and the gold prize from the Society of Illustrators Los Angeles.

한림 단편소설 시리즈를 기획하고 제작한 스튜디오 바프는 책의 컨셉에서부터 제작에 이르는 북프로듀싱의 전 과정을 관장하며 책의 기획에 부합하는 일관성 있는 디렉션을 통해 글과 그림과 디자인을 아우르는 일을 전문으로 하고 있다. 다수의 출판사와 기업, 미술관의 책을 기획하여 프로듀싱한 바 있다. The Hollym Short Story Series was planned and produced by studio BAF, experts in combining literary works with illustrations and designs in a manner that matches specific project goals, who oversee the entire process from conceptualization to production. They have worked on projects and produced books for numerous publishing companies, businesses and art museums in Korea for over 10 years.

굽이굽이 외지기만 한 그 산길을
저 아그 발자국만 따라 밟고 왔더니라······.

Along the winding lonesome mountain road,
I only followed his footprints in the snow....

1

"내일 아침 올라가야겠어요."

점심상을 물러나 앉으면서 나는 마침내 입 속에서 별러 오던 소리를 내뱉아 버렸다.

노인과 아내가 동시에 밥숟가락을 멈추며 나의 얼굴을 멀거니 건너다본다.

"내일 아침 올라가다니. 이참에도 또 그렇게 쉽게?"

노인은 결국 숟가락을 상 위로 내려놓으며 믿기지 않는다는 듯 되묻고 있었다.

나는 이제 내친걸음이었다. 어차피 일이 그렇게 될 바엔 말이 나온 김에 매듭을 분명히 지어 두지 않으면 안 되었다.

"예, 내일 아침에 올라가겠어요. 방학을 얻어 온 학생 팔자도 아닌데 남들 일할 때 저라고 이렇게 한가할 수가 있나요. 급하게 맡아 놓은 일도 한두 가지가 아니고요."

"그래도 한 며칠 쉬어 가지 않고……난 해필 이런 더운 때를 골라 왔길래 이참에는 며칠 좀 쉬어 갈 줄 알았더니……"

"제가 무슨 더운 때 추운 때를 가려 살 여유나 있습니까."

1

"We have to leave tomorrow morning."

As I was leaving the breakfast table, I finally managed to blurt out the sentence that I had been contemplating for some time.

Both my mother and my wife stopped eating and gazed at me blankly.

"Leave tomorrow morning?" my mother echoed in mild shock, as if she could not believe her own ears. She laid her spoon on the table. "You're leaving so soon this time also."

I decided to clarify my statement, realizing that I had already spilled the beans.

"Yes. I'm not a student on vacation, you know. I can't afford to be idle while others are working hard. Besides, I have a few urgent projects to be taken care of in the office."

"I understand." my mother said. "I wish you

"그래도 그 먼 길을 이렇게 단걸음에 되돌아가기야 하겠냐. 넌 항상 한동자로만 왔다가 선걸음에 새벽길을 나서곤 하더라마는……이번에는 너 혼자도 아니고……하룻밤이나 차분히 좀 쉬어 가도록 하거라."

"오늘 하루는 쉬었지 않아요. 하루를 쉬어도 제 일은 사흘을 버리는 걸요. 찻길이 훨씬 나아졌다곤 하지만 여기선 아직도 서울이 천릿길이라 오는 데 하루 가는 데 하루……."

"급한 일은 우선 좀 마무리를 지어 놓고 오지 않구선……."

노인 대신 이번에는 아내 쪽에서 나를 원망스럽게 건너다보았다. 그건 물론 나의 주변머리를 탓하고 있는 게 아니었다. 내게 그처럼 급한 일이 없다는 걸 그녀는 알고 있었다.

서울을 떠나올 때 급한 일들은 미리 다 처리해 둔 것을 그녀에게는 내가 말을 해 줬으니까. 그리고 이번에는 좀 홀가분한 기분으로 여름 여행을 겸해 며칠 동안이라도 노인을 찾아보자고 내 편에서 먼저 제의를 했었으니까. 그녀는 나의 참을성 없는 심경의 변화를 나무라고 있는 것이었다.

그리고 그 매정스런 결단을 원망하고 있는 것이었다. 까닭 없는 연민과 애원기 같은 것이 서려 있는 그녀의 눈길이

눈길 11

could stay here a few more days and get some rest. Since you came down at the peak of this hot weather, I'd hoped you'd stay a few days this time."

"Do you believe I have the luxury of choosing between hot and cold weather?" I complained.

"Must you go back so soon? It is such a long trip back. Do you really have to leave right away? You used to come alone and return at the crack of dawn. I remember it well. But this time you didn't come alone. Please stay one more night and catch up on your needed rest before you leave."

"Well, Mother, I'll enjoy a good rest all day long today. You should know by now that one day's rest means three lost working days for me."

Although travel had been considerably improved, it took a tremendous amount of time to go back and forth between Seoul and my mother's house—one whole day to get to her house and another day to go back to Seoul.

"I wish you'd take care of urgent matters in the office before you come." my mother said.

This time, my wife, not my mother, looked at me with eyes full of reproach, which indeed had nothing to do with my incompetence in handling office affairs. My wife knew well that no urgent business matters were awaiting my return.

Right before we left Seoul, I told my wife that I had already taken care of every important matter. It was I who suggested to my wife that we take our summer vacation in a relaxed manner this year. It was also me who suggested to her that we visit my mother for a few days during our vacation.

My wife was casting resentful looks at me because of my hasty change of plans, reproaching me for my cold decision to leave my mother's

그것을 더욱 분명히 하고 있었다.

"그래, 일이 그리 바쁘다면 가 봐야 하기는 하겠구나. 바쁜 일을 받아 놓고 온 사람을 붙잡는다고 들을 일이겠나."

한동안 입을 다물고 앉아 있던 노인이 마침내 체념을 한 듯 다시 입을 열어 왔다.

"항상 그렇게 바쁜 사람인 줄은 안다마는, 에미라고 이렇게 먼 길을 찾아와도 편한 잠자리 하나 못 마련해 주는 내 맘이 아쉬워 그랬던 것 같구나."

말을 끝내고 나서는 무연스런 표정으로 장죽 끝에 풍년초를 꾹꾹 눌러 담기 시작한다.

너무도 간단한 체념이었다.

담배통에 풍년초를 눌러 담고 있는 그 노인의 얼굴에는 아내에게서와 같은 어떤 원망기 같은 것도 찾아볼 수가 없었다. 당신 곁을 조급히 떠나고 싶어하는 그 매정스런 아들에 대한 아쉬움 같은 것도 엿볼 수가 없었다.

성냥불도 붙이려 하지 않고 언제까지나 그 풍년초 담배만 꾹꾹 눌러 채우고 앉아 있는 노인의 눈길은 차라리 무표정에 가까운 것이었다.

나는 그 너무도 간단한 노인의 체념에 오히려 불쑥 짜증

home so suddenly. I could clearly detect this. Yet her gaze also reflected both a pity and a pleading that I could not interpret.

"Well, then, if you're that busy, you ought to go back." my mother said. "It won't do any good to hold back a busy person like you. I know you won't listen to me no matter how hard I try to dissuade you from leaving!"

My mother then remained mute for a while, as if she had finally given up trying to convince me not to go.

"I know you're always busy," she finally said. "Try and understand where I'm coming from, though. You came all the way down here to see me, yet I couldn't even provide you with a comfortable bed. Please try to understand why I wanted you to stay longer."

My mother began to tamp cheap tobacco into her long pipe. She seemed resigned to my

이 치솟았다.

나는 마침내 자리를 일어섰다. 그리고는 그 노인의 무표정에 밀려나기라도 하듯 방문을 나왔다.

장지문 밖 마당가에 작은 치자나무 한 그루가 한낮의 땡볕을 견디고 서 있었다.

2

지열이 후끈거리는 뒤꼍 콩밭 한가운데에 오리나무 무성한 묘지가 하나 있었다. 그 오리나무 그늘에 숨어 앉아 콩밭 아래로 내려다보니 집이라고 생긴 게 꼭 습지에 돋아 오른 여름 버섯 형상을 닮아 있었다.

나는 금세 어디서 묵은 빚문서라도 불쑥 불거져 나올 것 같은 조마조마한 기분이었다.

애초의 허물은 그 빌어먹게 비좁고 음습한 단칸 오두막 때문이었다. 묵은 빚이 불거져 나올 것 같은 불편스런 기분이 들게 해 오는 것도 그랬고, 처음 예정을 뒤바꿔 하루 만에 다시 길을 되돌아갈 작정을 내리게 한 것 역시 그러했다.

decision, with no trace of the resentment on her face that I had noted in my wife just a few minutes before. She showed no hard feelings toward her heartless son who was anxious to leave his mother in such a hurry. Without bothering to light a match for her pipe, her face was expressionless.

It was now I who was suddenly provoked by her apparent resignation. Annoyed, I stood up briskly. I then left the room in a haste, as if I were pushed out by my mother's expressionless stare. At the edge of the front courtyard near the sliding lattice door, I noticed a small jasmine tree, enduring the scorching sun of noontide.

2

Behind the house was a grave under the thick-

leaved alder tree in the midst of a bean patch that was being baked by the intense heat. Taking a seat under the shade of the alder tree, where I was almost hidden, I looked down at my mother's one-room hut through the bean bushes. The shape of the house reminded me of a summer mushroom sprouting in a marsh.

I feared that a belated demand for payment of an old debt would emerge suddenly from nowhere at any minute. That dim, humid and tiny one-room hut was to blame in the first place. It was the hut that aroused this terrible sense of nervousness in me. It forced me to feel that my old debt might reappear. It was indeed my mother's hut that had led me to change my mind, deciding to return to Seoul after only one day's stay.

To begin with, I owed nothing to my mother. I prided myself on having a debt-free relationship with her. Consequently, I had nothing to hide from her. My mother's sentiment, of course, was the same about the matter of any debt existing between us.

Noticing that her teeth were completely decayed, I once made a casual suggestion to my mother that I purchase an inexpensive set of dentures for her, as she had a terribly difficult time chewing. But my mother must have doubted my ability to pay for even a cheap set of dentures; she declined my well-intentioned offer right then and there.

"I'm approaching my seventies," she said. "I don't think I have that much time left."

Another time, I recommended she have an operation for her hemorrhoids, which had worsened in her old age. She was in pain whenever she had to go to the bathroom.

"Thank you, son, but no." She refused to hear

anything further. "I'll go to the other world as I am now. I'm all right. I don't expect any comfort at my age anyway." My mother voiced a reply to my offer very similar to the one concerning the dentures.

"I may be an old woman, but I'm still a decent woman. I can't bring myself to expose my private parts to a stranger. I'd rather endure discomfort until my time comes."

It was evident that she had given up on the remainder of her life. She was convinced that she would not live much longer. More precisely, however, my mother felt that she had neither a right to demand nor to receive anything in return from her own son. That much was at least clear to me.

I was in the ninth grade when my older brother, a hopeless alcoholic, brought bankruptcy upon our family due to his excessive drinking habits.

하지만 내게 빚은 없었다. 노인에 대해선 처음부터 빚이 있을 수 없는 떳떳한 처지였다.

노인도 물론 그 점에 대해선 나를 완전히 신용하고 있었다.

"내 나이 일흔이 다 됐는데, 이제 또 남은 세상이 있으면 얼마나 길라더냐."

이가 완전히 삭아 없어져서 음식 섭생이 몹시 불편스러워진 노인을 보고 언젠가 내가 지나가는 말처럼 권해 본 일이 있었다. 싸구려 가치라도 해 끼우는 게 어떻겠느냐는 나의 말선심에 애초부터 그래 줄 가망이 없어 보여 그랬던지 노인은 단자리에서 사양을 해 버리는 것이었다.

"이럭저럭 지내다 이대로 가면 그만일 육신, 이제 와 늘그막에 웬 딴 세상을 보겠다고……."

한번은 또 치질기가 몹시 심해져서 배변이 무척 힘들어하시는 걸 보고 수술 같은 걸 권해 본 일도 있었다.

노인은 그때도 역시 비슷한 대답이었다.

"나이를 먹어도 아녀자는 아녀자다. 어떻게 남의 눈에 궂은 데를 보이겠더냐. 그냥 저냥 참다 갈란다."

남은 세상이 얼마 길지 못하리라는 체념 때문에도 그랬겠지만, 그보다 노인은 아무것도 아들에겐 주장하거나 돌려받

When he finally died, he left three small children and his wife to fend for themselves. He also left me a sense of duty because I then became the eldest son in the household.

The relationship between my mother and myself had been like this ever since my brother's death. My mother had not assumed any parental responsibility for me during my high school and college years, or even during my three years of service in the army. Nor had I assumed any filial responsibility toward her.

Even after I was discharged from the army, I did not dare take up the role of eldest son toward my mother, not because she did not deserve such treatment, but because I just could not afford to do so. In the long run, I ended up neglecting the responsibility that my deceased brother had left for me to assume. I had no choice but to neglect my duty as the eldest son in the family.

을 것이 없는 당신의 처지를 감득하고 있는 탓에도 그리 된 것이었다.

고등학교 1학년 때 형의 주벽으로 가계가 파산을 겪은 뒤부터, 그리고 마침내 그 형이 세 조카아이와 그 아이들의 홀어머니까지를 포함한 모든 장남의 책임을 내게 떠맡기고 세상을 떠난 뒤부터 일은 줄곧 그렇게만 되어 온 셈이었다.

고등학교와 대학교와 군영 3년을 치러 내는 동안 노인은 내게 아무것도 낳아 기르는 사람의 몫을 못 했고, 나는 또 나대로 그 고등학교와 대학과 군영의 의무를 치르고 나와서도 자식놈의 도리는 엄두를 못 냈다. 노인이 내게 베푼 바가 없어서가 아니라 그럴 처지가 못 되었기 때문이다. 나는 나대로 형이 내게 떠맡기고 간 장남의 책임을 감당하기를 사양치 않을 수가 없었기 때문이었다.

노인과 나는 결국 그런 식으로 서로 주고받을 것이 없는 처지였다. 노인은 누구보다 그것을 잘 알고 있었다. 그렇기 때문에 내게 대해선 소망도 원망도 있을 수가 없었다.

그런 노인이었다. 한데 이번에는 웬일인지 노인의 눈치가 이상했다. 글쎄 그 가치나 수술마저 한사코 사양을 해 온 노인이, 나이 여든에서 겨우 두 해가 모자란 늘그막에 와서야

That is why my relationship with my mother was one in which nothing was ever given or received. My mother knew it well, more than anyone else, which is why she could not nurture any hope or harbor any resentment toward me. Such, I thought, was our understanding.

This time, however, I detected a somewhat different attitude in my mother, the same woman who had once flatly refused my help to obtain dentures or to undergo an operation. My mother, only two years shy of eighty now, was in the twilight of her life. All of a sudden, though, she must have had a certain renewed appetite for life. I suspected she was dreaming an impossible dream. It was, indeed, a preposterous dream. "The Movement for the Replacement of Old Roofs" was the beginning of the trouble.

"Every house in the village has had its roof replaced with either tiles or plastic slates," my

새삼스레 다시 딴 세상 희망이 생긴 것일까.

노인은 아무래도 엉뚱한 꿈을 꾸고 있는 것 같았다. 그것은 너무나 엄청난 꿈이었다.

지붕 개량 사업이 애초의 허물이었다.

"집집마다 모두 도단 아니면 기와들을 얹는단다."

노인은 처음 남의 말을 하듯이 집 이야기를 꺼냈었다. 어제 저녁때 노인과 셋이서 잠자리를 들기 전이었다. 밤이 이슥해서 형수는 뒤늦게 조카들을 데리고 이웃집으로 잠자리를 얻어 나가 버리고, 우리는 노인과 셋이서 그 비좁은 오두막 단칸방에다 잠자리를 함께 폈다.

어기영차, 어기영! 그때 어디선가 밤일을 하는 남정들의 합창 소리가 왁자하게 부풀어 올랐다. 귀를 기울이고 듣고 있다가 무슨 소리냐니까 노인이 문득 생각난 듯이 귀띔을 해 왔다.

"동네가 너도나도 집들을 고쳐 짓느라 밤잠들을 안 자고 저 야단들이구나."

농어촌 지붕 개량 사업이라는 것이었다. 통일벼가 보급된 후로는 집집마다 그 초가지붕 개초가 어렵게 되었단다. 초봄부터 시작된 지붕 개량 사업은 그래저래 제격이었다. 지

mother had said offhandedly, as if she were merely gossiping. This happened last night right before the three of us—my mother, my wife and myself—went to bed. As night deepened, my sister-in-law and her children went to sleep at a neighbor's house. After they left, the three of us took out the bedding and prepared to go to sleep in that tiny one-bedroom hut.

It was then we heard the night workers' chorus—"hi-ho, hi-ho"—resounding loudly from somewhere not very far away. I strained my ears with curiosity, trying to make out the sounds. I asked my mother to explain what was going on.

"Everyone in the village is remodeling their house, as if they're competing with one another," my mother explained lightly, like she had just happened to remember it. "They work through the night, making such a fuss."

According to my mother, the people in the

village were doing their part to improve their old roofs, honoring the campaign of roof improvement throughout the farming and fishing villages.

Since unification, it had been very difficult for the villagers to replace their roofs with either tiles or slates because of poor harvests. My mother informed us that rice seeds had been distributed by the government throughout the entire village.

The ambitious task of replacing the old roofs had been going rather well in every aspect since early spring. My mother explained that if anyone completed his roof according to strict regulations, he would receive fifty thousand *won* from the government as a subsidy. My mother went on to say that most of the villagers replaced their roofs during the slack season, right before and right after the period of transplanting rice seedlings into the rice paddies.

When I was first told all about this movement,

my heart sank deeply. At that moment, the idea of owing something to my mother popped into my head. What if she nurtured a futile hope for her dream of a better life? I managed to overcome my anxiety, however, when I realized that my mother would not demand anything hasty or unreasonable from a son like myself. Even if she did nurture the impossible hope of a new roof for her house, it was out of the question due to the condition of her hut. To begin with, the house was not strong enough to hold the weight of new tiles or slates on the roof.

I suspected my mother knew this fact, and so therefore did not harbor any hope for the improvement. The way she talked about it gave me the impression that she was merely referring to someone else's business. I eventually found out that I was wrong, though, and that I had misunderstood her all along. Her deep, inner

붕을 개량하면 정부 보조금 5만 원을 얻는다는 것이었다. 모심기가 시작되기 전 봄철 한때하고 모심기가 끝난 초여름께부터 지금까지 마을 집들 거의가 일을 끝냈단다.

나는 처음 그런 노인의 이야기를 들었을 때 무턱대고 가슴부터 덜렁 내려앉고 있었다. 노인에 대한 빚 생각이 처음으로 머릿속에 떠오른 순간이었다. 이 노인이 쓸데없는 소망을 지니면 어쩌나. 하지만 나는 곧 마음을 가라앉혔다. 무엇보다도 나는 노인에 대해서 빚이란 게 없었다. 노인이 그걸 잊었을 리 없었다. 그리고 그런 아들에게 섣부른 주문을 내색할 리 없었다. 전부터도 그 점만은 안심을 할 만한 노인의 성깔이었다. 한데다가 그 노인이 설령 어떤 어울리잖을 소망을 지닌다 해도 이번에는 그 집 꼴이 문제 밖이었다. 도대체가 기와고 도단이고 지붕을 가꿀 만한 집 꼴이 못 되었다. 그래저래 노인도 소망을 지녀 볼 엄두를 못 낸 모양이었다. 이야기하는 말투가 영락없는 남의 일이었다.

하지만 사실은 그게 오해였다. 노인의 속마음은 그게 아니었다.

"관에서 하는 일이라면 이 집에도 몇 번 이야기가 있었겠군요?"

thoughts were quite different from mine.

"If this movement is sponsored by the local government, I'm sure you've been told about it several times." I made this insensitive remark out of over-optimism. Soon, however, I realized my mistake. My mother got up from her bedding and began to fill her long pipe with a pinch of cheap tobacco over her pillow.

"What makes you think my house was excluded?" my mother said in a matter-of-fact voice, as if she were still conveying somebody's message. "The head of our village came and pressed me to go along with the movement. The men from the town office came by and even threatened me. This happened once or twice. In the end, however, the authorities changed their tactics by pleading for my help, so to speak."

"How did you manage to keep feeding them excuses, Mother?" I asked. I still could not figure

사태를 너무 낙관한 나머지 위로 겸해 한마디 실없는 소리를 내놓은 것이 나의 실수였다.

　노인이 다시 자리를 일어나 앉았다. 그리고 머리맡에 놓아 둔 장죽 끝에다 풍년초 한 줌을 쏘아 박기 시작했다.

　"왜 우리 집이라 말썽이 없었더라냐."

　노인은 여전히 남의 말을 옮기듯 덤덤히 말했다.

　"이장이 쫓아와 뜸을 들이고, 면에서 나와서 으름장을 놓고 가고……그런 일이 한두 번뿐이었으면야……나중엔 숫제 자기들 쪽에서 사정조로 나오더라."

　"그래 어머닌 뭐라고 우겼어요?"

　나는 아직도 노인의 진심을 모르고 있었다.

　"우길 것도 뭣도 없는 일 아니겠냐. 지놈들도 눈깔이 제대로 박힌 인간들일 것인디……사정을 해 오면 나도 똑같이 사정을 했더니라. 늙은이도 사람인디 나라고 어디 좋은 집 살고 싶은 맘이 없겠소. 맘으로야 천 번 만 번 우리도 남들같이 기와도 입히고 기둥도 갈아 내고 하고는 싶지만 이 집 꼴을 좀 들여다보시오들, 이 오막살이 흙집 꼴에다 어디 기와를 얹고 말 것이 있겠소……."

　"그랬더니요?"

눈길　33

out what she was really thinking.

"There's nothing to make excuses about," she replied. They have eyes for themselves to see with. If they pleaded with me, I did the same. I told them that even if I am an old woman, I am a human being who has a desire to live in better conditions. I told them I'd love to have my roof replaced with new tiles. I also told them I'd love to have new pillars, even if it could only be done in my imagination. I invited them to look closely at my hut. I told them the house is nothing but a hut made of clay. How can anyone put tiles on the roof?" I asked.

"And then what happened?"

"Well, after that, they came a few more times. Then they stopped coming and nagging altogether. They must have figured out what pathetic conditions I live in. They're not so stupid as not to notice the degree of poverty I endure.

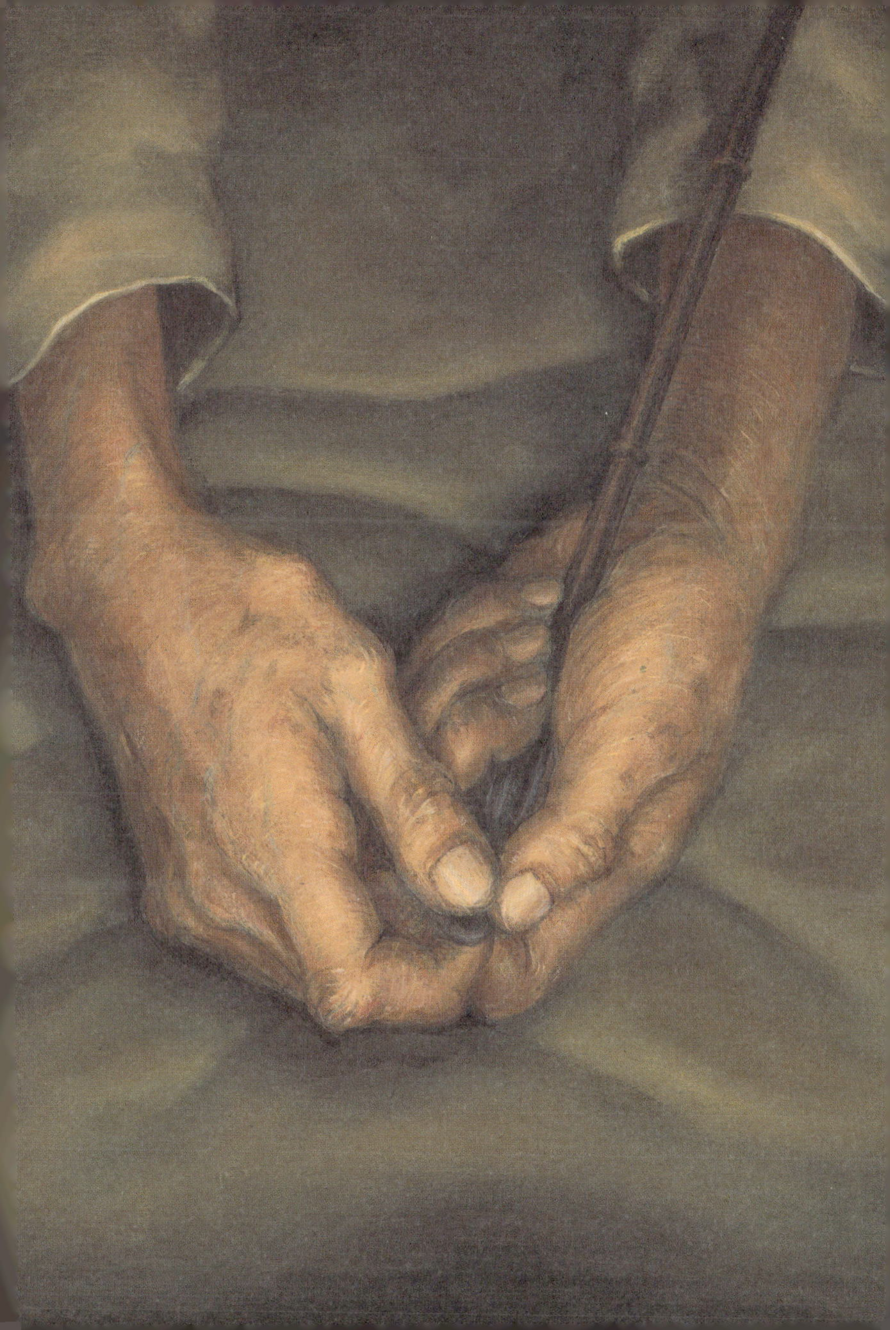

Once they saw my house, they knew." My mother stopped talking and pushed down on the end of the hot pipe with her calloused, weather-beaten thumb tip.

"I bet the villagers wanted an exemplary village after completing the roof replacement one hundred percent," I said uncomfortably, hoping to end the conversation. But again, I miscalculated.

"Incidentally, the authorities said the same thing as you just did," my mother replied. "After they finish the house they're working on tonight, all the houses in the village will be completed except two, mine and Sun-sim's, down the road."

"Nonetheless, do you really think the authorities will keep hounding you to put new tiles on your roof just because they're anxious to make this village a model for the sake of the movement?"

"I don't know. If they asked me only to replace

"그랬더니 몇 번 더 발길을 스쳐 가더니 그 담엔 흐지부지 말이 없더라. 지놈들도 이 집 꼴을 보면 사정을 모를 청맹과니들이라더냐?"

노인은 그 거칠고 굵은 엄지손가락 끝으로 장죽 끝을 눌러 대고 있었다.

"그 친구들 아마 이 동네를 백 퍼센트 지붕 개량으로 모범 마을을 만들고 싶어 그랬던 모양이군요."

나는 왠지 기분이 씁쓸하여 그런 식으로 그만 이야기를 얼버무려 넘기려고 하였다. 그런데 그게 오히려 결정적인 실수였다.

"하기사 그 사람들도 그런 소리들을 하더라. 오늘 밤일을 하고 있는 저 집 일을 끝내고 나면 이제 이 동네에서 지붕 개량을 안 한 집은 우리하고 저 아랫동네 순심이네 두 집밖에 안 남는다니까 말이다."

"그래도 동네 듣기 좋은 모범 마을 만들자고 이런 집에까지 꼭 기와를 얹으라 하겠어요."

"글쎄 말이다. 차라리 지붕에 기와나 도단만 얹으랬으면 우리도 두 눈 딱 감고 한 번 저질러 보고 싶기도 하더라마는, 이런 집은 아예 터부터 성주를 다시 할 집이라 그렇

the roof, I would be tempted to comply with their wishes. However, this house needs to be rebuilt. It needs stronger pillars to support the tiles."

Somehow the conversation had strayed from its original subject. Realizing this, my heart sank once again as it was too late to change the topic.

"The core of this movement is replacing the roof," my mother continued, "but some people have taken advantage of this opportunity and actually remodeled their houses."

My mother went on to tell me in detail about what was happening in the village. Listening to her, I realized that this movement had indeed mushroomed. Its initial purpose was to replace the thatched roofs with either tiles or slates, yet as the task proceeded, a number of people found their houses structurally unable to hold the weight of the tiles. In order to sustain the weight of a new tile roof, they had to replace the old

제……."

 모범 마을이 꼬투리가 되어서 이야기가 다시 엉뚱한 곳으로 번지고 있었다. 나는 비로소 다시 가슴이 섬짓해 왔다. 하지만 이미 때가 너무 늦고 말았다.

 "하기사 말이 쉬운 지붕 개량이제 알속은 실상 새 성주를 하는 집도 여러 집 된단다."

 한 번 이야기를 꺼낸 노인이 거기서부터는 새삼 마을 사정을 소상하게 털어놓기 시작했다.

 그 지붕 개량 사업이라는 것은 알고 보니 사실 융통성이 꽤나 많은 일이었다. 원칙은 그저 초가지붕을 벗기고 기와나 도단을 얹는 것이었지만, 기와의 하중을 견뎌 내기 위해선 기둥을 몇 개쯤 성한 것으로 갈아 넣어야 할 집들이 허다했다. 그걸 구실로 대부분의 사람들은 성주를 새로 하듯 집들을 터부터 고쳐 지어 버렸다. 노인에게도 물론 그런 권유가 여러 번 들어 왔다. 기둥이 허술해서 기와를 못 얹는다는 건 구실일 뿐이었다. 허술한 기둥을 구실로 끝끝내 기와 얹기를 미뤄 온 집이 세 가구가 있었는데 이날 밤에 또 한 집이 새 성주를 위해서 밤일을 벌이고 있다는 것이었다. 노인이 기와 얹기를 단념한 것은 집 기둥이 너무 허해서가 아니

pillars.

Using this as an excuse, the majority of the villagers ended up remodeling their houses by expanding the original foundation. My mother was asked to do the same. The poor condition of the old pillars was just an excuse, they felt. In the beginning, just three households persisted in not complying with the flow of the movement, using their shoddy pillars as an excuse. One of these three families, however, gave in and was working on the new foundation tonight. My mother added that they would work through the night.

I did not believe my mother's refusal to put new tiles on the roof stemmed from the need for new pillars. It was rather from her fear of also needing a new foundation which I believe had made her abandon the idea altogether.

I could not, as yet, afford to be optimistic about this situation. Suddenly, I was enveloped once

었다. 노인은 새 성주가 겁이 나 일을 단념할 수밖에 없었던 것이다.

 허술한 기둥만 믿을 수는 없었다.

 일은 아직도 낙관할 수 없었다. 나는 불시에 다시 그 노인에 대한 나의 빚만을 생각하고 이었다.

 노인도 거기서 한동안은 그저 꺼져 가는 불에만 신경을 쏟고 있는 것 같았다. 하더니 이윽고는 더 이상 소망을 숨기기가 어려운 듯 가는 한숨을 삼키는 것이었다. 그러고는 그 한숨 끝에다 무심결인 듯 덧붙이고 있었다.

 "이참에 웬만하면 우리도 여기다 방 한 칸쯤이나 더 늘여 내고 지붕도 도단으로 얹어 버리면 싶긴 하더라만……."

 마침내 노인이 당신의 소망을 내비친 것이었다.

 "오늘 당할지 낼 당할지 모를 일이기는 하다만, 날짐승만도 못한 목숨이 이리 모질기만 하다 보니 별의별 생각이 다 드는구나. 저런 옷궤 하나도 간수할 곳이 없어 이리 밀치고 저리 밀치다 보면 어떤 땐 그저 일을 저질러 버리고 싶은 생각이 꿀떡 같아지기도 하고……."

 노인은 결국 그런 식으로 당신의 소망을 분명히 해 버리고 만 셈이었다. 지금은 아니더라도 적어도 그런 소망을 지

again with a sense of concern. Perhaps I did owe something to my mother. As I was lost in thought, my mother seemed to shift her interest to the waning glow in her tobacco pipe.

"This time the town office people let it go without making a big deal about it," my mother began again, seemingly talking to herself since I gave her no response whatsoever. "Anyway, I wonder if they'll be as lenient with me next year as they have been so far. I don't like to think that I'd comply with their wishes out of fear. Nonetheless, think of your nephews, niece, and your sister-in-law. They may not like to sleep with me in the same room. Even though there is enough space, every night they go to a neighbor's place to sleep. Perhaps they can't stand the smell of an old woman. I just can't ignore their sleeping at someone else's house."

Listening to my mother, I could detect a

considerable, detailed agenda of plans that had already been filed in her head.

"The government will offer fifty thousand *won* as a subsidy, mind you," she continued. "If I decided to go along with the movement, I doubt I would have to spend a great deal of money just to finish the roof. I realize I might have a hard time finding workers since I have no male adult members in my household, unlike the other families. However, if your sister-in-law promised to work in the fields during the summer for the neighbor right across from my house, I don't think the man there could entirely ignore our labor problem. I'm sure he'd help us."

My mother added that she could ask this neighbor for help doing the clay work, too. She could also ask about buying timber for new pillars from the head of the village at a bargain price since he owned the valley.

The glow of her pipe had now died away. She kept on puffing the extinguished pipe as she talked about how difficult it was for her to give up the government subsidy of fifty thousand *won* and the would-be help from the neighbors, but she gave no sign of dissatisfaction with me. In fact, she asked nothing from me.

She discussed all this as if it had taken place long ago and she was merely expressing idle thoughts. She was certainly not expecting her desire to become a reality. But I could tell that my mother was going out of her way not to relieve me of any sense of burden as she silently puffed on the cold pipe. Finally, she heaved a gentle sigh, like she was having difficulty in repressing her hidden desire any longer.

"If I took this opportunity, I'd be tempted to add an extra room and replace the old roof with slates," she then said, sighing again. "I don't

녔던 것만은 분명히 한 것이었다.

나는 이제 할 말이 없었다. 눈을 감은 채 듣고만 있었다. 노인에 대해선 빚이 없음을 골백 번 속으로 다짐하고 있었다.

"이번에는 면에서도 그냥 흐지부지 지나가 주더라만 내년엔 또 이번처럼 어떻게 잠잠해 주기나 할는지. 하기사 면 사람들 무서워 집을 고친다고 할 수도 없지마는, 늙은이 냄새가 싫어 그런지 그래도 한데서 등짝 붙이고 누울 만한 방 놔두고 밤마다 남의 집으로 잠자릴 얻어 다니는 저것들 에미 꼴도 모른 체하지는 못할 일이니라."

내가 아예 대꾸를 않으니까 노인은 이제 혼잣말 비슷이 푸념을 계속했다. 듣다 보니 그 노인의 머릿속엔 상당히 구체적인 계획표까지 이미 마련되어 있었던 것 같았다.

"나라에서 보조금을 5만 원이나 내주겠다. 일을 일단 저지르고 들었더라면 큰돈이야 얼마나 더 들 일이 있었을라더냐……. 남정네가 없어 남들처럼 일손을 구하기가 쉽진 않았겠지만 네 형수가 여름 한철만 밭을 매 주기로 했으면 건넛집 용석이 아배라도 그냥 모른 체 하지는 않았을 것이다……."

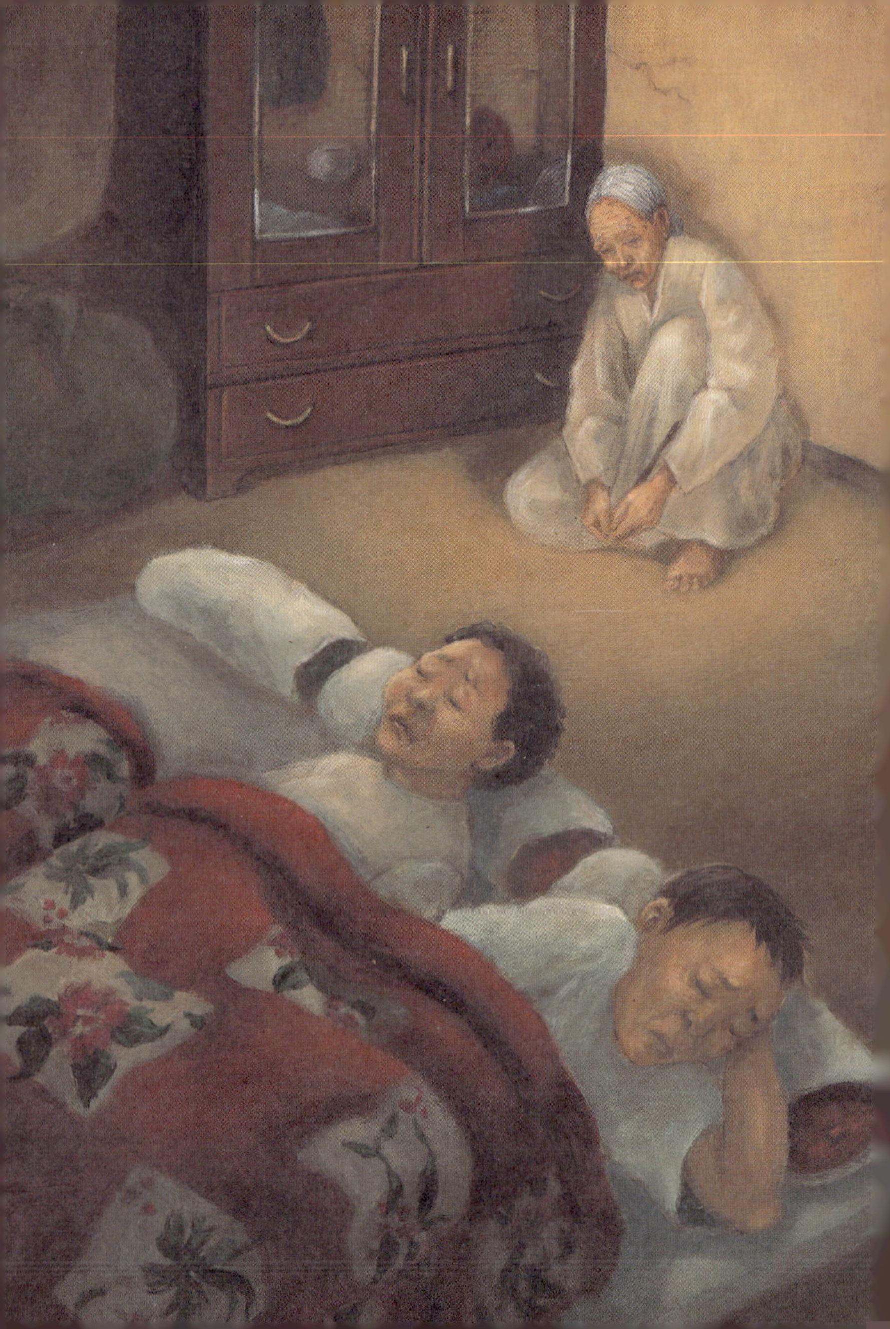

흙일을 돌볼 사람은 그 용석이 아버지에게 부탁을 하고 기둥을 갈아 낼 나무 가대는 이장네 산에서 헐값으로 몇 개를 부탁해 볼 수가 있었다는 것이었다.

 노인의 장죽 끝에는 이제 불기가 꺼져 식어 있었다.

 노인은 연신 그 불이 꺼진 장죽을 빨아 대면서, 한사코 그 보조금 5만 원과 이웃의 도움이 아까워서라도 일을 단념하기가 아쉬웠다는 투였다.

 하지만 노인은 그러면서도 끝끝내 내게 대한 주장이나 원망의 빛을 보이진 않았다. 이야기의 형식은 어디까지나 과거의 일로서 그런 생각을 해 봤을 뿐이고, 그럴 뻔했다는 말일뿐이었다. 그리고 그런 식으로 나에 대해선 어떤 형식으로도 직접적인 부담감을 느끼게 하지 않으려는 식이었다. 말하는 목소리도 끝끝내 그 체념기가 짙은 특유의 침착성을 잃지 않은 채였다.

 "하지만 다 소용없는 일이다. 세상일이 그렇게 맘 같이만 된다면야 나이 먹고 늙은 걸 설워 안 할 사람이 있으라더냐. 나이를 먹으면 애기가 된다더니 이게 다 나이 먹고 늙어 가는 노망기 한가지제."

 종당에는 그 당신의 은밀스런 소망조차도 당신 자신의 실

눈길 47

know when I'll die. Perhaps today or tomorrow. Anyway, my life, of no more worth than that of a wild animal, seems to be long. My head is now crowded with wild notions." It was then that my mother at last disclosed her inner desire. "I don't have a room for even a single dresser," she continued. "Whenever I see the dresser being pushed from one place to another, I'm tempted to carry out my desire to add a room and put on a new roof."

My mother succeeded by this unique method in revealing with crystal clarity her innermost hope. She apparently had felt such a desire at one time, but surely she did not cherish it now. I did not know what to say. I was in bed, listening to her with my eyes closed, reminding myself again and again that I owed nothing to my mother. To the end, she successfully maintained a most unique tone of absolute resignation.

"It's all useless," my mother said softly. "If the world ran as smoothly as one desired, who wouldn't be sorry about getting old! I have heard people say the old are like children. Perhaps I am becoming too old. I think like a child now."

In the end, my mother blamed her old age and hopeless senility on her secret, innermost desire. Despite this, there was no way for me to fail to discern her thoughts. Even my wife, listening to my mother without stirring in her bed while she pretended to sleep, must have clearly recognized my mother's real wish.

When my wife brought a basin full of water for me to wash my face and hands the next morning, she asked me reproachfully, "Couldn't you have said something nicer to your mother last night?" I threw a scowling, harsh glance in her direction as a message not to put her nose where it didn't belong. Unaffected by my glare, my wife

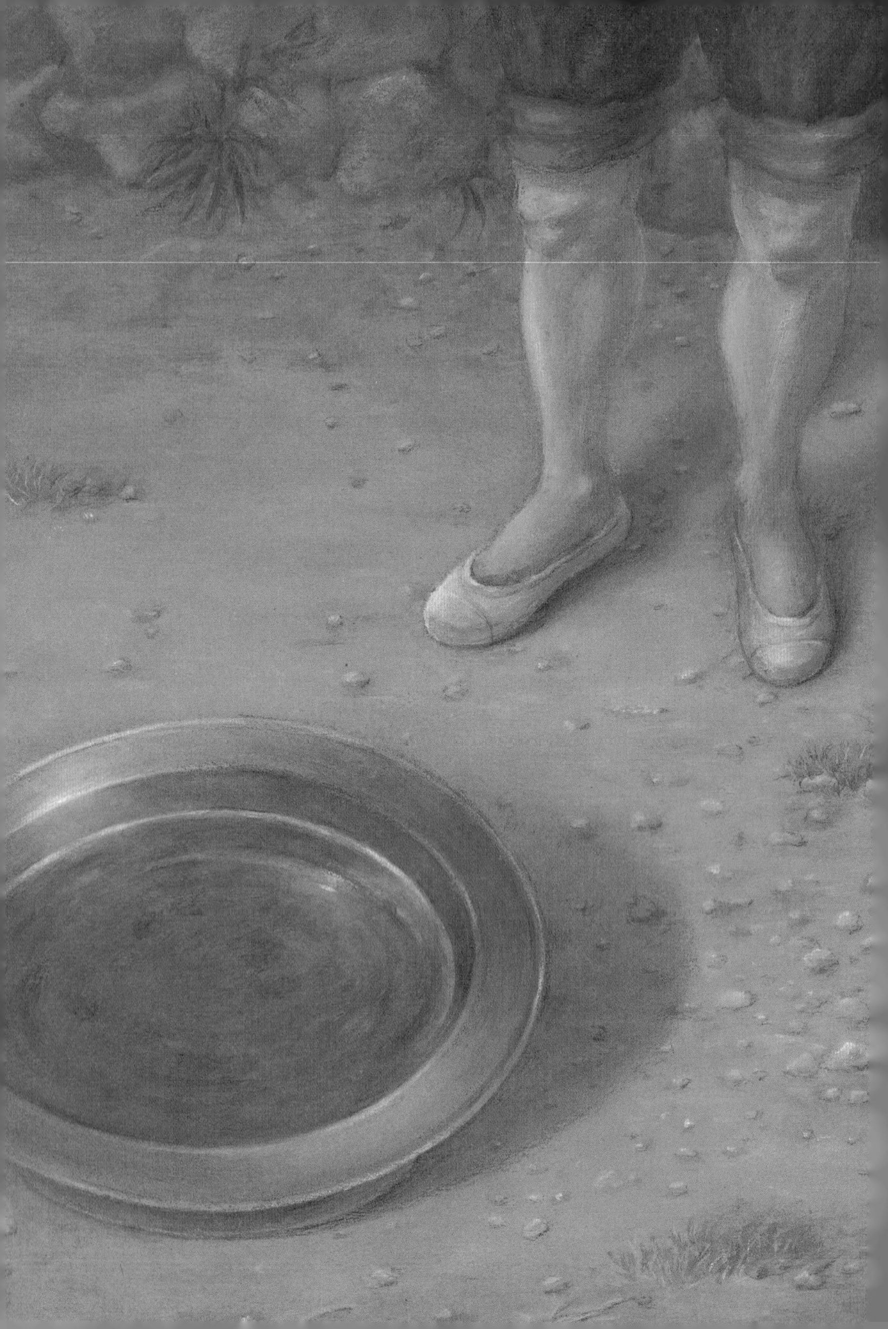

없는 노망기 탓으로 돌려 버리고 있었다.

하지만 나는 이제 노인의 내심을 못 알아볼 리 없었다. 한마디 말참견도 없이 눈을 감고 잠이 든 체 잠잠히 누워만 있던 아내까지도 그것을 분명히 눈치 채고 있었다.

"당신, 어젯밤 어머니 말씀에 그렇게 밖에 응대해 드릴 방법이 없었어요?"

오늘 아침 아내는 마당가로 세숫물을 떠 들고 나왔다가 낮은 소리로 추궁을 해 왔다. 그때 나는 아내에게 그저 쓸데없는 참견 말라는 듯 눈매를 잔뜩 깎아 떠 보였었다. 하니까 아내는 그러는 나를 차라리 경멸조로 나무라고 있었다.

"당신은 참 엉뚱한 데서 독해요. 늙은 노인네가 가엾지도 않으세요. 말씀이라도 좀 더 따뜻하게 위로를 드릴 수 있었을 텐데 말예요."

아내도 분명 노인의 말뜻을 알아듣고 있었다. 그리고 나보다도 노인의 일을 걱정하고 있었다. 노인에 대한 나의 속마음도 속속들이 모두 읽고 있을 게 당연했다. 내일 아침으로 서둘러 서울로 되돌아가겠노라는 나의 결정에 아내가 은근히 분개하고 나선 것도 그런 사연을 모두 알고 있었기 때문이었다. 한다고 그년들 무슨 뾰족한 수가 있을 수가 있는가.

눈길 51

proceeded to reprimand me harshly.

"You're so cruel!" she cried. "How could you find it in your heart to be so aloof? Don't you feel sorry for your old mother? You could have at least said something comforting to her!"

It was clear that my wife understood exactly what my mother had tried to convey to me. She was more concerned about my mother than I was. I was sure that my wife had already sensed in detail all of the deepest thoughts I had concerning my mother. My wife's earnest anger toward my decision to return to Seoul the next morning in such a hurry was mainly because she knew and understood how shamefully I had treated my mother.

In any event, what could she have done to change things? I wondered. It seemed clear that my mother wished to have her house remodeled. I could not fathom her reasoning. I wondered

어쨌든 노인이 이제라도 그 집을 새로 짓고 싶어하고 있는 건 분명했다. 아무래도 알 수가 없는 일이었다. 아닌게아니라 나이를 먹으면 노인들은 모두 어린애가 되어 가는 것일까. 노인은 정말로 내게 빚이 없다는 사실을 잊어버리고 만 것일까. 노인의 말처럼 그건 일테면 노망기가 분명했다. 그런 염치도 못 가릴 정도로 노인은 그렇게 늙어 버린 것이었다. 하지만 나는 굳이 노인의 그런 노망기를 원망할 필요도 없었다. 문제는 서로 간의 빚의 문제였다. 노인에 대해 빚이 없다는 사실만이 내게는 중요했다. 염치가 없어져서건 노망을 해서건 노인에 대해 내가 갚아야 할 빚만 없으면 그만인 것이었다.

―빚이 있을 리 없지. 절대로! 글쎄 노인도 그걸 알고 있으니까 정면으로는 말을 꺼내지 못하질 않던가 말이다.

어디선가 무덥고 게으른 매미 울음소리가 들리고 있었다.

나는 비로소 자신을 굳힌 듯 오리나무 그늘에서 몸을 힘차게 일으켜 세웠다. 콩밭 아래로 흘러 뻗은 마을이 눈앞으로 멀리 펼쳐져 나갔다. 거기 과연 아직 초가지붕을 이고 있는 건 노인네의 그 버섯 모양의 오두막과 아랫동네의 다른 한 채가 전부였다.

how she could forget that I was not indebted to her for anything at all. As my mother suggested earlier, she must indeed have entered into a state of senility. Is it really true that an old person transforms into a baby?

My mother had apparently aged so much that she was unable to distinguish between pride and honor. I had no reason to feel any guilt because of her senility. The only important thing for me to remember was that I owed her nothing. Whether she became brazen or senile, I did not care. All that mattered was keeping my position of being debt-free to my mother.

I owe her nothing. Nothing! I reassured myself. That's why Mother has no heart to ask me directly for her desire to remodel her house. I know she knows that I'm debt-free to her.

As I was thinking about this, I heard the steady, lazy cries of the cicada from somewhere. As if reinforced with confidence, I stood up resolutely from the shady spot beneath the alder tree.

Below the bean patch, the panorama of the entire village came into focus, a bird's-eye view from the hill where I stood. As my mother said, the only thatched roofs in the village belonged to her mushroom-shaped hut and another house down the road.

Disturbed, I cursed the improvement program: "Damn it! Why is the government making such a fuss over this program of improving roofs at a time like this!"

3

Quite some time after the sun sank, I climbed down the hill, crossed the bean patch and walked into the backyard of my mother's house.

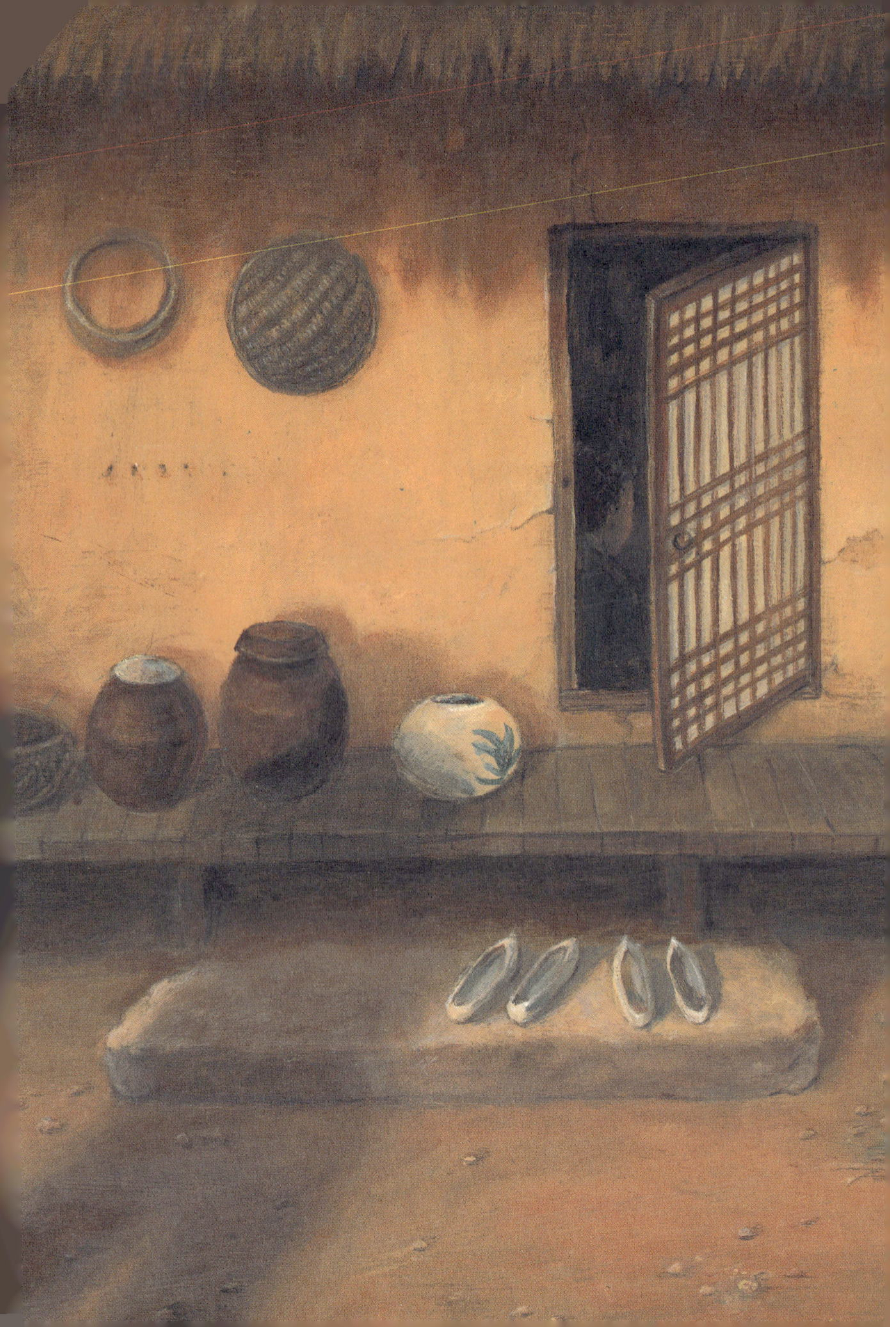

―빌어먹을! 그 지붕 개량 사업인지 뭔지 하필 이런 때 법석들이지?

아무래도 심기가 편할 수는 없었다. 나는 공연히 그 지붕 개량 사업 쪽에다 애꿎은 저주를 보내고 있었다.

3

해가 훨씬 기운 다음에야 콩밭을 가로질러 노인의 집 뒤꼍으로 뜰을 들어서려다 보니, 아내는 결국 반갑지 않은 화제를 벌여 놓고 있었다.

"이 나이에 내가 살면 얼마나 더 좋은 세상을 살겠다고 속없이 새 방들이고 기와 지붕을 덮자겠냐……집 욕심 때문이 아니라 나 간 뒷일이 안 놓여 그런다……."

뒤꼍에서 안뜰로 발길을 돌아서려는데, 장지문을 반쯤 열어젖힌 안방에서 노인의 말소리가 도란도란 흘러나오고 있었다.

"날씨가 신선한 봄 가을철이나, 하다못해 마당에 채일(차일)이라도 치고들 지내는 여름철만 되더라도 걱정이 덜하겠

"I'm not expecting to live very long," my mother was saying to my wife. "Of course, I don't expect such a thing as a comfortable life at my age. I didn't mean to have my roof replaced with tiles or add an extra room just for my sake. I suppose my wish was too unreal. I'm worried about the titles after I die. I'm not greedy just because I want to have things done before my time, am I? I'd just like to do something for my place."

As I was about to enter the front courtyard, my mother's low voice could be faintly heard from the room through the half-open sliding lattice door. I was overhearing a conversation that I instinctively knew I would rather not hear.

"If it were considerably cooler in the spring or fall, or even if it were cooler in the summertime, when people can sleep under a canopy in the courtyard, I wouldn't be so much concerned," my

다마는, 한겨울 추위 속에서나 운 사납게 숨이 딸깍 끊어져 봐라. 단칸방 아랫목에다 내 시신 하나 가득 늘어놓으면 그 일을 어찌할 것이냐."

이번에도 또 그 집에 관한 이야기였다. 노인을 어떻게 위로한다는 것일까. 아니면 아내는 노인의 소망을 더 이상 어떻게 외면할 수가 없도록 노골화시켜 버리고 싶었던 것일까.

답답하게 눈치만 보고 도는 내게 대한 아내의 원망은 그토록 뿌리가 깊고 지혜로왔더란 말인가. 노인의 이야기는 아내가 거기까지 유도해 내고 있었던 게 분명했다. 노인은 이제 그 아내 앞에 당신의 집에 대한 소망을 분명한 목소리로 털어놓고 있었다.

그리고 이젠 당신의 소망에 대한 솔직한 사연을 말하고 있었다. 노인의 그 오랜 체념의 습관과 염치를 방패삼아 어물어물 고비를 지나가려던 내 앞에 노인의 소망이 마침내 노골적인 모습을 드러내 온 것이었다. 노인의 소망은 이미 짐작하고 있었지만, 설마하면 그렇게 분명한 대목까지는 만나게 될 줄을 몰랐던 일이었다. 나는 마치 마지막 희망이 무너진 느낌이었다. 하지만 그 노인의 설명에는 나에게도 마침내 분명해진 것이 있었다. 노인이 갑자기 그 집에 대한 엉

mother went on. "However, what if I die in the dead of winter—which would be just my luck. My daughter-in-law and her children would have no choice but to keep my body in the upper part of the only room we have in the house. What would they do in that situation?"

So my mother was still talking about the house! And was my wife's anger toward me so deep because I had behaved so objectionably and remained so aloof? Was that why she was shrewd enough to talk to my mother herself behind my back? It was plain to me that my wife had managed to succeed in leading my mother to continue talking. Now my mother was wholeheartedly expressing her wish about the house right in front of my wife, who must have won my mother's trust. My mother was now unveiling the story behind her wish. The transparency of her desire was presented right before my eyes, when I was all ready to pass by it one way or another. I felt that her resignation had become a long-time habit, believing this shielded me against any sense of shame.

Although I had guessed her wish long before, I was quite unprepared for hearing this very clear statement from her. I watched the last ray of hope disappear. There was one thing about her statement that clarified things for me at last. This was her own personal reason for her sudden and preposterous desire to improve her house. My mother was not motivated by the idea of enjoying a new comfortable life for herself, but for those who would be left behind after her death.

"Even though I came here as an outsider, I've spoken ill of no one nor have I hurt anyone in this village to this day. I've lived in this decent way all of my life," my mother went on with my wife.

"I can't deny that I have been leading an extremely meager life. As you can see, I'm still living in dire poverty. Nonetheless, no one in the neighborhood has said anything unkind to me. I have come this far, keeping a decent relationship with my neighbors. Do you understand what I'm trying to say, my dear? After I die, the villagers will come to the burial ground either to cast a shovelful of dirt on my coffin or to put some grass on my grave. I'm sure that is the least they would do for me. Who would prevent these mourners, regardless of age, young or old, from paying their last respects to me? There is nothing more tiring for people than fulfilling their duties after someone's death. No one can prevent people from paying their last respects, especially to an old woman who has known nothing but poverty all her life."

She sighed deeply and continued. "Do you

뚱한 소망을 지니게 된 당신의 내력이었다. 노인은 아직도 당신의 삶을 위해서는 새삼스런 소망을 지니지 않고 있었다. 노인의 소망은 당신의 사후에 내력이 있었다.

"떠돌아 들어 살아오긴 했어도, 난 이 동네 사람들한테 못할 일은 한 번도 안 해 보고 살아 온 늙은이다. 궂은 밥 먹고 궂은 옷 입고 궂은 잠자리 속에 말년을 보냈어도 난 이웃이나 이 동네 사람들한테 궂은 소리는 안 듣고 늙어 왔다. 이 소리가 무슨 소린고 하니 나 죽고 나면 그래도 이 동네 사람들, 이 늙은이 주검 위에 흙 한 삽, 뗏장 한 장씩은 덮어주러 올 거란 말이다. 늙거나 젊거나 그렇게 날 들여다봐 주러 오는 사람들을 어찌할 것이냐. 사람은 죽어서 고단해지는 것보다 더 고단한 것도 없는 법인디, 오는 사람 마다할 수 없고 가난하게 간 늙은이가 죽어서라도 날 들여다봐 주러 오는 사람들한테 쓴 소주 한잔을 대접해 보내고 싶은 게 죄가 될 거나. 그래서 그저 혼자서 궁리해 본 일이란다. 숨 끊어지는 날 바로 못 내다 묻으면 주검하고 산 사람들이 방 하나뿐 아니냐. 먼 데서 온 느그들도 그렇고……그래서 꼭 찬바람이나 막고 궁둥이 붙여 앉을 방 한 칸만 어떻게 늘여 봤으면 했더니라마는……그게 어디 맘 같은 일이더냐. 이도 저

눈길 63

believe it's a crime for me to want to treat these mourners with just a glass of cheap whiskey? That's why, I suppose, I came up with this wild idea after considerable thinking. When I take my last breath of life, if my body cannot be buried the same day, it will be a big problem. You see, the body and the rest of the family have to stay in the same room. Besides that, what about you and my son who will come such a long distance? That's the reason I had this notion to have an extra room added in any way I could manage. I just need a small room that can shield us from the cold wind and hold a small person like me. Anyway, my wish has stayed only in my heart this whole time. I guess it was nothing but a futile hope of a senile old woman. I must be living in a fantasy world. Do you think I am?"

My mother's wish, I realized, had originated as preparation for her own death.

도 다 늙고 속없는 늙은이의 노망길 테제……."

 노인의 소망은 바로 그 당신의 죽음에 대한 대비에서 비롯된 것이었다.

 알 만한 노릇이었다. 살림이 망하고 옛 살던 동네를 나와 떠돌기 시작하면서부터 언제나 당신의 죽음에 대한 대비를 게을리 해 오지 않던 노인이었다. 동네 뒷산 양지바른 언덕 아래다 마을 영감 한 분에게 당신의 집터(노인은 당신의 무덤 자리를 늘 그렇게 말했다)를 미리 얻어 놓고 겨울철에도 날씨가 좋으면 그곳을 찾아가 햇볕 바래기를 하다가 내려온다던 노인이었다. 노인은 이제 당신의 죽음에 마지막 준비를 서두르고 있는 것이었다. 나는 아무래도 더 노인의 이야기를 엿듣고 있을 수가 없었다. 발길을 움직여 소리 없이 자리를 피해 버리고 싶었다.

 한데 그때였다. 쓸데없는 일에 공연히 감동을 잘하는 아내가 아무래도 견딜 수가 없어진 모양이었다.

 "전에 사시던 집은 터도 넓고 간수도 많았다면서요?"

 아내가 느닷없이 화제를 바꾸고 나섰다. 별달리 노인을 달랠 말이 없으니까, 지나간 일이나마 그렇게 넓게 살던 옛집의 기억을 상기시켜서라도 노인을 위로하고 싶어진 것이

Ever since she was forced to leave her own village and wander from one village to another after the family's bankruptcy, my mother had been obsessed with the idea of making preparations for her own death. She had already secured a gravesite (she called it a homesite) from a certain elderly man in this present village. It was located on a sunny side of the foot of the mountain that overlooked the village. She often went to her gravesite to bask in the sun on a fine day, even in wintertime. I could tell she was now making precise final preparations for her imminent death.

I found myself feeling awkward. I wanted to leave the spot as quietly as I possibly could. But as I was about to take a step to leave the place, I overheard a remark of my wife's that changed the subject abruptly.

"I understand your previous house was big and

built on a huge lot." Perhaps she could not control her curiosity any longer; or perhaps she was desperate to find something to comfort my mother and happened to think of this statement. She might have wanted my mother to reminisce over the fond memory of having the spacious house that she once enjoyed and thus somehow be consoled.

Also, my wife, always with the best intentions, undoubtedly sensed my mother's shame at revealing her obvious poverty to her daughter-in-law. Recalling her former position might soothe my mother's injured pride to some degree.

I found the need to leave diminished for the time being.

"My old house was spacious. Very, very big, actually," I overheard my mother say. "It was enormous. The front and back yards put together were as big as a regular playground. Well, it doesn't matter now. It was all for nothing. Someone else has lived in that house now for more than twenty years."

"I know how you must feel, Mother," my wife said. "I'm sure your fond memories about your big, splendid house stay in your heart. You can recall those fine, happy days whenever you feel irritated or depressed about your present house."

"What's the use of recalling the memory? Whenever I think of those bygone years, my already troubled heart becomes even more burdened. I don't need to relive such memories now."

"You may be right, Mother. I don't blame you for becoming more irritable in your present living conditions whenever your memory returns to those days in such a huge house. I feel bad that you have ended up living in a tiny, one-room hut."

리라. 그것은 노인도 한때 번듯한 집 살림을 해 온 기억을 되돌이키게 해서 기분을 바꿔 드리고 싶어서이기도 했겠지만, 그 외에도 그것은 또 언제나 가난한 살림만을 보고 가게 하는 부끄러운 며느리 앞에 당신의 자존심을 얼마간이나마 되살려 내게 할 가외의 효과도 있을 수 있었다. 어쨌거나 나는 당분간 다시 자리를 피할 필요가 없어지고 있었다.

"옛날 살던 집이야, 크고 넓었제. 다섯 간 겹집에다 앞뒤 터가 운동장이었더니라……하지만 이제 와서 그게 다 무슨 소용이냐. 남의 집 된 지가 20년이 다 된 것을……."

"그래도 어머님은 한때 그런 좋은 집도 살아 보셨으니 추억은 즐거운 편이 아니시겠어요? 이 집이 답답하고 짜증나실 땐 그런 기억이라도 되살려 보세요."

"기억이나 되살려서 어디다 쓰게야. 새록새록 옛날 생각이 되살아나다 보면 그렇지 않아도 심사가 어지러운 것을."

"하긴 그것도 그러실 거예요. 그렇게 넓은 집에 사셨던 생각을 하시면 지금 사시는 형편이 더 짜증스러워지기도 하시겠죠. 뭐니 뭐니 해도 지금 형편이 이렇게 비좁은 단칸방 신세가 되고 마셨으니 말씀예요……."

노인과 아내는 잠시 그렇게 위론지 넋두린지 분간이 가지

Was the intent of their conversation to complain or to comfort? As I listened to them go on, I began once again to doubt my wife's true motives. I could tell by the tone of her voice that she was not trying to comfort my mother. She was, in fact, provoking my mother, whose heart had become subsequently more troubled.

My wife was indeed fanning my mother's guarded desire to remodel the house by forcing her to expose that desire. I now believed this was my wife's intention. My first assumption concerning my wife's motives was turning out to be not so terribly wrong.

"By the way, Mother, why don't you move this dresser out of the room and store it elsewhere? It takes up too much space in this tiny room." My wife, at last, led the subject into a most uncomfortable matter, which I had been avoiding to this day: it was the story behind the dresser.

It was either seventeen or eighteen years ago, when I was in my first year of high school. My brother's heavy drinking habits worsened as each day passed. He sold every rice paddy and vegetable field we owned. He even sold the mountain that we had inherited from our ancestors. My brother sold everything we had in order to support his alcoholism. One day I heard a rumor that my brother sold our house as a last resort. We had lived in that house since my father's generation.

At the time, I was living in a nearby city and spending my winter vacation there. I could not stand not knowing what in the world was going on back home. In order to appease this nagging curiosity, I went back to the village. According to the rumor, the house had already been sold.

Consequently, I did not expect to find any member of my family in the house and so had no place to go to find out their whereabouts.

I waited until dusk gathered before I actually entered the street where I used to live, only to discover that the rumor was in fact true. The house was completely empty. No one was around. I left and went to see a distant relative who lived nearby. According to my relative, my mother was still waiting for me in the house, which was unexpected news.

"Why are you acting like this on your own street? Where do you think you are? This is your house, remember?" my mother reproached me when I had finally reached the house. I appeared to be hesitant, not knowing how to behave near the house. I was standing awkwardly near the gate when she came up to me. She must have somehow heard about my visit to my distant relative.

I followed my mother inside, still clinging to

않는 소리들을 주고받고 있었다. 한동안 그렇게 오가는 이야기를 듣다 보니, 나는 그 아내의 동기가 다시 조금씩 의심스러워지고 있었다. 아내의 말투는 그저 노인을 위로하기 위해서가 아니었다. 노인을 위로해 드리기커녕은 심기만 점점 더 불편스럽게 하고 있었다. 노인에게 옛집을 상기시켜 드리는 것은 당신의 불편스런 심기를 주저앉히기보다 오늘을 더욱 더 비참스럽게 느끼게 만들고 있었다. 집을 고쳐 짓고 싶은 그 은밀스런 소망을 자꾸만 밖으로 후벼대고 있었다. 아내의 목적은 차라리 그쪽에 있었던 것 같았다.

아내에 대한 나의 판단은 과연 크게 빗나가지 않고 있었다.

"방이 이렇게 비좁은데 그럼 어머니, 이 옷장이라도 어디 다른 데로 좀 내놓을 순 없으세요? 이 옷장을 들여놓으니까 좁은 방이 더 비좁지 않아요."

아내는 마침내 내가 가장 거북스럽게 시선을 피해 오고 있는 곳으로 화제를 끌어들이고 있었다.

바로 그 옷궤 이야기였다. 17, 8년 전, 고등학교 일 학년 때였다. 술버릇이 점점 사나와져 가던 형이 전답을 팔고 선산을 팔고, 마침내는 그 아버지 때부터 살아 온 집까지 마지막으로 팔아넘겼다는 소식이 들려왔다. K시에서 겨울 방학

unfounded optimism. My last ray of hope dissipated, however, when I sensed that our house had been sold as I entered the main wing of the house. On that evening, my mother prepared a meal for me as she used to. She and I spent the night there, and she sent me back to the city at the break of dawn.

Later I managed to find out that my mother had secured permission from the new owner of the house for her to fix dinner for me and have me spend one last night in our house. She had been awaiting my visit to our house so that she could carry out her wish for my sake. I suspected she wanted me to sleep, even if for one last night, in our own house, so that I would feel comfortable in a familiar environment.

Although a strangeness in the air told me the house had been sold, my mother was keeping it mopped and dusted. My mother's dresser and

을 보내고 있던 나는 도대체 일이 어떻게 되어 가는지 알아보고 싶어 옛 살던 마을을 찾아가 보았다. 집을 팔아 버렸으니 식구들을 만나게 될 기대는 없었지만, 그래도 달리 소식을 알아 볼 곳이 없었기 때문이었다. 어스름을 기다려 살던 집 골목을 들어서니 사정은 역시 K시에서 듣고 온 대로였다. 집은 텅텅 비어진 채였고 식구들은 어디론지 간 곳이 없었다. 나는 다시 골목 앞에 살고 있던 먼 친척 간 누님을 찾아갔다. 그런데 그 누님의 말을 들으니, 노인이 뜻밖에 아직 나를 기다리고 있다는 것이었다.

"여기가 어디냐. 네가 누군데 내 집 앞 골목을 이렇게 서성대고 있어야 하더란 말이냐."

한참 뒤에 어디선가 누님의 소식을 듣고 달려온 노인이 문간 앞에서 어정어정 망설이고 있는 나를 보고 다짜고짜 나무랐다. 행여나 싶은 마음으로 노인을 따라 문간을 들어섰으나 집이 팔린 것은 분명해 보였다.

그날 밤 노인은 옛날과 똑같이 저녁을 지어 내왔고, 그날 밤을 거기서 함께 지냈다. 그리고 이튿날 새벽 일찍 K시로 나를 다시 되돌려 보냈다. 나중에야 안 일이었지만 노인은 그렇게 나에게 저녁 밥 한 끼를 지어 먹이고 마지막 밤을 지

눈길 75

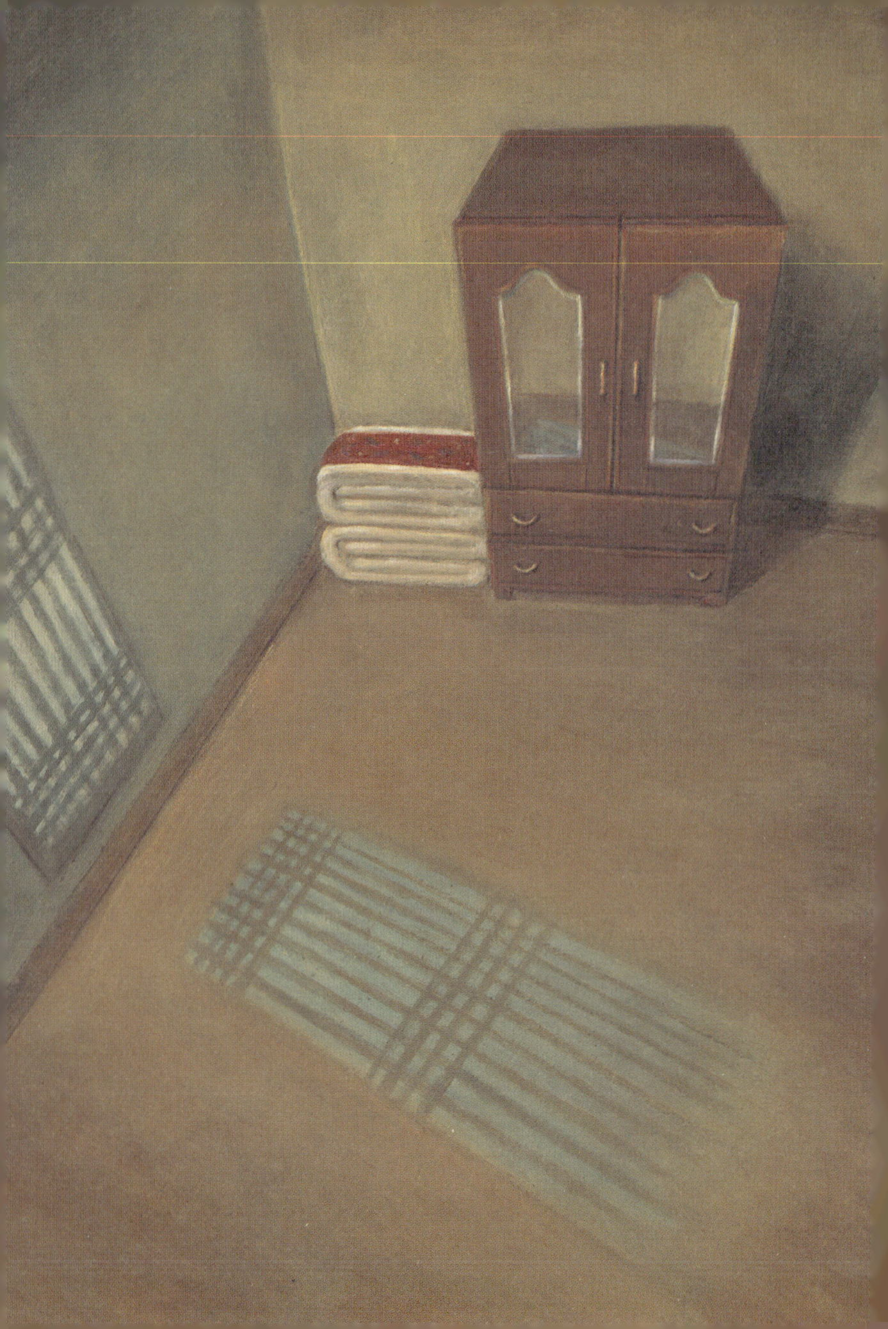

내게 해 주고 싶어, 새 주인의 양해를 얻어 그렇게 혼자서 나를 기다리고 있었다는 것이었다. 언젠가 내가 다녀갈 때까지는 하룻밤만이라도 내게 옛집의 모습과 옛날의 분위기 속에 자고 가게 해 주고 싶어서였는지 모른다. 하지만 문간을 들어설 때부터 집안 분위기는 이사를 나간 빈집이 분명했었다.

한데도 노인은 그때까지 매일같이 그 빈집을 드나들며 먼지를 떨고 걸레질을 해 온 것이었다. 그리고 그때 노인은 아직 집을 지켜 온 흔적으로 안방 한쪽에다 이불 한 채와 옷궤 하나를 예대로 그냥 남겨 두고 있었다.

이튿날 새벽 K시로 다시 길을 나설 때서야 비로소 집이 팔린 사실을 분명히 해 온 노인의 심정으로는 그날 밤 그 옷궤 한 가지로나마 옛집의 분위기를 되살려 나의 괴로운 잠자리를 위로하고 싶었음이 분명한 것이었다.

그러한 내력이 숨겨져 온 옷궤였다.

떠돌이 살림에 다른 가재도구가 없어서도 그랬겠지만, 이 20년 가까이를 노인이 한사코 함께 간직해 온 옷궤였다. 그만큼 또 나를 언제나 불편스럽게 만들어 온 물건이었다. 노인에게 빚이 없음을 몇 번씩 스스로 다짐하고 있다가도 그

눈길 77

simple bedding remained in the same corner of the main bedroom.

At dawn, when I was ready to leave for the city, my mother finally told me in her clear tone of voice that our house was sold. It was evident that she wanted to comfort me and believed in her heart that the mere existence of the chest in the room might help me recall the atmosphere of our old house to which I was accustomed.

My mother had now been storing the dresser ever since, for nearly twenty years. I believed the reason for this was the scarcity of her belongings as she had to keep moving from one place to another. The dresser always made me feel uncomfortable, though. While I could firmly convince myself that I owed my mother nothing, whenever I looked at the dresser, I felt very awkward, as if I were facing an indebtedness I did not intend to acknowledge.

Such was the dresser to me.

On this visit, the dresser succeeded in making me feel this way again. The first moment I walked into my mother's room, the sight of the dresser caused me a great sense of discomfort. The deep root of my final decision to leave for Seoul after only one day's stay, I reasoned, was due to the dresser.

I had told my wife the history of this dresser several times. If my wife understood its meaning, I was confident she would understand how I felt about it. Moreover, if she knew I could overhear their conversation near the room, she would surely be even more sympathetic to my feelings. Even so, I found myself so tense that I nearly resorted to my old habit of picking my nose to calm myself.

I was seized with tension. I was afraid of suddenly encountering a debt popping out of nowhere. My mother might attack in her shameful way, cornering me with the dilemma of admitting this old debt.

"You can do whatever you like. Even if you insist, I am sure I owe you nothing. Not a thing! You might try desperately, Mother, but it's useless. Nothing can make me believe I owe you anything. I am debt-free." I closed my eyes as if I were praying and recited these words over and over. And I waited.

Again, I overheard my mother replying to my wife.

"If I move the dresser somewhere else, where would we keep our clothing?" My mother was talking in her usual matter-of-fact, almost casual, tone. Somehow this relieved my anxiety.

"Besides, we have no other place to store the dresser."

"You could hang your clothes on nails from the

옷궤만 보면 무슨 액면가 없는 빚문서를 만난 듯 몹시 기분이 꺼림칙스러워지곤 하던 물건이었다.

이번에도 물론 마찬가지였다. 노인의 방에 들어선 순간에 벌써 기분을 불편스럽게 해 오던 옷궤였다. 그리고 끝내는 이틀 밤을 못 넘기고 길을 다시 되돌아갈 작정을 내리게 한 것도 알고 보면 바로 그 옷궤의 허물이 컸을지 모른다.

아내도 물론 그 옷궤에 관한 내력을 내게서 들을 만큼 듣고 있었다.

아내가 옷궤의 내력을 알고 있는 여자라면, 그 옷궤에 관한 나의 기분도 짐작을 못할 그녀가 아니었다. 더욱이 내가 바깥에서 두 사람의 이야기를 엿듣고 있는 걸 알고서 그랬을 수도 있었다.

나는 어느새 그 콧속을 후비는 못된 버릇이 되살아날 만큼 긴장을 하고 있었다. 생각지도 않았던 곳에서 갑자기 묵은 빚문서가 튀어나올 것 같은 조마조마한 기분이었다. 노인이 치사하게 그 묵은 빚문서로 나를 궁지에 몰아넣으려 덤빌 수도 있었다.

—그래 보라지. 누가 뭐래도 내겐 절대로 빚진 게 없으니까. 그래본들 없는 빚이 생길 리가 있을라구.

눈길 81

wall," my wife suggested. "Most of all, a person needs space to lie down with their legs fully stretched out. It appears to me that you value the dresser more than the well-being of people."

My wife's bold remark was obviously intended to test my mother's deep attachment to the dresser. In spite of my wife's urging, however, my mother responded in her usual manner.

"I'm afraid you don't know what you're talking about. If I didn't have the dresser, who could ever tell this is a house with someone living in it? It belongs right here in the house. Don't you see that it testifies to the presence of people?"

"I bet you must have some kind of meaningful, hidden story about your dresser," my wife teased. "Did you buy it when you were first married?"

My mother was old enough to be my wife's grandmother, and yet my wife acted and talked rather disrespectfully around her, like she were a

나는 거의 기구를 드리듯 눈을 감고 기다렸다.

하지만 다행스러운 것은 아직도 그 무심스러워 보이기만 한 노인의 대꾸였다.

"옷궤를 내놓으면 몸에 걸칠 옷가지는 다 어디다 간수하고야? 어디다 따로 내놓을 데가 있는 것도 아니지만, 그걸 어디다 내놓을 데가 생긴다고 해도 그것말고는 옷가지 나부랑일 간수해 둘 데는 있어얄 것 아니냐."

알고 그러는지 모르고 그러는지 노인은 그리 그 옷궤 쪽에는 신경을 쓰고 있지 않은 것 같았다.

"옷이야 어떻게 못을 박아 걸더라도, 사람이 우선 좀 발이라도 뻗고 누울 자리가 있어야잖아요. 이건 뭐 사람들보다도 옷장을 모시는 꼴이지 뭐예요."

아내는 거의 억지를 부리고 있었다.

옷궤에 대한 노인의 집착심을 시험해 보기 위한 수작임이 분명했다.

하지만 노인의 반응은 여전히 의연했다.

"그건 네가 모르는 소리다. 그 옷궤라도 하나 없으면 이 집을 누가 사람 사는 집이라 할 수 있겠냐. 사람 사는 집 흔적으로 해서라도 그건 집안에 지녀야 할 물건이다."

눈길 83

privileged granddaughter. This time, however, my wife was even mischievous.

"What story, my dear, could you be talking about?" My mother seemed not to wish to talk about the dresser any more.

"How did your house come to be sold, Mother?" my wife pressed.

"What kind of question is that? I didn't sell it in the spirit of playing a game. I suppose I'm just not destined to have my own house." My mother did not have the slightest idea that my wife knew all about the reason for the sale of the house.

"But, Mother, there must have been some reason why you had to sell your house," my wife insisted. "I understand your husband went to a lot of trouble to have that house built, and died while it was under construction."

"You're right, my dear. We acquired the house only after going through a lot of hard times. You

"어머님은 아마 저 옷장에 그럴 만한 사연이 있으신가 보군요. 시집오실 때 해 오신 건가요?"

노인의 나이가 너무 높다 보니 아내는 때로 그 노인 앞에 손주딸처럼 버릇이 없어지기도 했지만, 이번에는 숫제 장난기 한가지였다.

"내력은 무슨……."

노인은 이제 그것으로 그만 입을 다물어 버리고 말았다. 옷궤 이야기는 더 이상 들추고 싶지가 않은 모양이었다.

하지만 아내도 이젠 그쯤에서 호락호락 물러설 여자가 아니었다. 노인이 입을 다물어 버리자 아내도 그만 거기서 할 말을 잃은 듯 잠시 침묵을 지키고 있더니 이윽고는 다시 공세를 펴기 시작했다.

"하긴 어쨌거나 어머님 마음이 편하진 못하시겠어요. 뭐니뭐니해도 옛날에 사시던 집을 지켜 오시는 게 최선이었는데 말씀예요. 도대체 그 집은 어떻게 해서 팔리게 되었어요?"

이번엔 또 그 집 얘기였다. 그 역시 모르고 묻는 소리가 아니었다. 아내는 그 옷궤의 내력과 함께 집이 팔리게 된 사정에 대해서도 모두 알고 있었다. 하면서도 그녀는 다시 노

눈길 85

see, the house was not built all at once as others were. We added one room at a time as our income increased in the course of many years. And now it has ended up in someone else's hands. Anyway, what's the use of talking about it now? I tell you the house was not meant for me. That's why the house went to somebody else. It's pointless to talk about it."

"I can see your point. But by the same token, you must be more acutely sorry about it since your house was made possible after such hardships, especially when you think of your present living conditions. Can you not tell me what really happened at the time, Mother? What really made you sell your house?"

"It doesn't matter. It's all futile. It was a long time ago, and my memory is not so good anymore."

My mother tried desperately not to yield to my

인에게 그것을 되풀이시키려 하고 있는 것이었다. 옷궤를 구실로 그 노인의 소망을 유인해 내려는 그녀 나름의 노력의 연장이었다.

하지만 노인의 태도도 아직은 그 아내에 못지않게 끈질긴 데가 있었다.

"집이 어떻게 팔리기는……안 팔아도 좋을 집을 장난삼아서 팔았을 라더냐. 내 집 지니고 살 팔자가 못 돼 그리된 거제……."

알고도 묻는 소릴 노인은 또 노인대로 내력을 얼버무려 넘기려고 하였다.

"그래도 사정은 있었을 게 아녜요? 그 집을 지을 때 돌아가신 아버님이 몹시 고생을 하셨다고 하던데요."

"집이야 참 어렵게 장만한 집이었지야. 남같이 한번에 지어 올린 집이 아니고 몇 해에 걸쳐서 한 간씩 두 간씩 살림 형편 좇아서 늘여 간 집이었더니라. 그렇게 마련한 집이 결국은 내 집이 못 되고……그런다고 어제 그런 소린 해서 다 뭣을 하겠냐. 어차피 내 집이 못 될 운수라 그리 된 일을 이런 소리 곱씹는다고 팔려 간 집 다시 내 집이 되어 돌아올 것도 아니고……."

wife's persistent efforts to entice her into telling the whole story.

"All right, Mother. You must be worried that your troubles might unnecessarily hurt me. Do you want to know the truth, though? I've known about your house all this time."

My wife was not the kind of woman to be discouraged and retreat just because of my mother's sudden silence. As my mother closed her mouth, my wife also remained silent for a few moments. Her silence, however, was short-lived.

"Anyway, Mother, I feel for you," my wife went on. "Your heart must be very troubled. You should have kept your old house at any cost. But I still don't know the story behind selling the house."

My wife's inquiry was not innocent. Just as she knew all about the history of my mother's dresser, my wife also had full knowledge of why the

"하지만 그리 어렵게 장만한 집이라 애석한 생각이 더할 게 아녜요. 지금 형편도 그럴 수밖에 없고요. 어떻게 되어 그리 되고 말았는지 그때 사정이라도 좀 말씀해 보세요."

"그만둬라, 다 소용없는 일이다. 이제는 그럭저럭 세월이 흘러서 기억도 많이 희미해진 일이고……."

한사코 이야기를 피하려는 노인에게 아내는 마침내 마지막 수단을 동원하고 있었다.

"좋아요. 어머님께선 아마 지난 일로 저까지 공연히 속을 상하게 할까 봐 그러시는 모양인데요, 그래도 별로 소용이 없으세요. 저도 사실은 이야기를 대강 다 들어 알고 있단 말씀예요."

"이야기를 들어? 누구한테서?"

노인이 비로소 조금 놀라는 기미였다.

"그야 물론 저 사람한테지요."

노인의 물음에 아내가 대답했다. 눈에는 보이지 않았지만, 밖에서 엿듣고 있는 나를 지목한 말투가 분명했다. 짐작대로 그녀는 벌써부터 내가 밖에서 엿듣고 있는 낌새를 알아차리고 있었음이 분명했다.

"제가 알고 있는 건 그 집을 팔게 된 사정 뿐만도 아니에

눈길 89

house had been sold. Still, she kept trying to have my mother repeat the whole story. She was trying to find out what lay behind my mother's desire, using the story of the house to achieve her scheme. My wife's persistent effort only drew out my mother's stubborn side.

"I know not only of the story behind the sale of your house, but I also know how you managed to have your son spend the last night in the house when it had already been sold. I know it all. I've been pretending that I knew nothing. I was told you still kept your worn-out dresser even to the last night in the house, trying to give your son the impression that you still lived there, as if nothing had happened."

"You heard? From whom?" my mother asked in a tone of mild shock.

"From him, of course," my wife replied. Although I had not been certain that my wife

요. 어머님께서 저 사람한테 그 팔려 간 집에서 마지막 밤을 지내게 해 주신 일도 모두 알고 있단 말씀예요. 모른 척하고 있기는 했지만 저 옷장 말씀예요, 그날 밤에도 어머님은 저 헌 옷장 하나를 집안에다 아직 남겨 두고 계셨더라면서요. 아직도 저 사람한텐 어머님이 거기서 살고 계신 것처럼 보이시려고 말씀이에요."

아내는 차츰 목소리가 떨려 나오고 있었다.

"그렇담 어머님, 이제 좀 속 시원히 말씀해 보세요. 혼자서 참아 넘기시려고만 하지 마시고 말씀이라도 하셔서 속을 후련히 털어 봐 보시란 말씀이에요. 저흰 어머님 자식들 아닙니까. 자식들한테까지 어머님은 어째서 그렇게 말씀을 참아 넘기시려고만 하세요."

아내의 어조는 이제 거의 울먹임에 가까웠다.

노인도 이젠 어찌할 수가 없는지, 한동안 묵묵히 대꾸가 없었다.

나는 온통 입안의 침이 다 마르고 있었다. 노인의 대꾸가 어떻게 나올지 숨도 못 쉰 채 당신의 다음 말만 기다리고 있었다.

하지만 그 아내나 나의 조바심하고는 아랑곳도 없이 노인

눈길 91

sensed my presence, at last I could tell for sure, since she was referring to me as "him." My wife, I guessed, had been aware of my presence all along.

"Please, Mother, tell me everything. Why don't you let it out once and for all? Why do you keep it all inside? We're your children. Why must you hide it from your children and bury everything in your heart?"

My wife sounded like she was near tears. My mother remained speechless for a good while as if she did not know what to say next. In the meantime, my mouth became extremely dry. I could not breathe properly while I waited, wondering if she were going to respond to my wife's plea.

Ignoring my wife's and my anguished waiting, however, my mother replied in a voice controlled to the end, "I wonder how he managed to

은 끝내 심기를 흩트리지 않았다.

"그래 그 아그(아이)도 어떻게 아직 그날 밤 일을 잊지 않고 있더냐?"

"그래요. 그리고 그날 밤 어머님은 저 사람이 집을 못 들어가고 서성대고 있으니까 아직도 그 집이 안 팔린 것처럼 저 사람을 안으로 데려다가 저녁까지 한 끼 지어 먹이셨다면서요."

"그럼 됐구나. 그렇게 죄다 알고 있는 일을 뭣 하러 한사코 나한테 되뇌게 하려느냐."

"저 사람은 벌써 잊어 가고 있거든요. 저 사람한테선 진짜 얘기를 들을 수도 없고요. 사람이 독해서 저 사람은 그런 일 일부러 잊어요. 그래 이번엔 어머님한테서 진짜 이야길 듣고 싶은 거예요. 저 사람 얘기 말고 어머님의 그날 밤 진짜 심경을 말씀이에요."

"심경이나마나 저하고 별다른 대목이 있었을 라더냐. 사세 부득해서 팔았다곤 하지만, 아직은 그래도 내 발길이 끊이지 않은 집인데, 그 집을 놔두고 그 아그가 그래 발길을 주춤주춤 어정대고 서 있더구나……."

아내의 성화를 견디다 못해 노인은 결국 마지못한 어조로

remember the last night in the house for this long...."

"But he does remember it. When he paced around the house, not knowing exactly what to do, you took him inside and even prepared a meal for him, trying to convince him that the house hadn't been sold."

"If you seem to know everything, my dear, why are you deliberately pressing so hard for me to recall and retell of those days?"

"Because he has already begun to forget about it. Besides, I'll never get the truth from him. He's so aloof that he willfully forgets things like that. I'd like to hear the truth from you personally this time. Not his version of the story, but your very own—your honest sentiments on that last night in your house."

"What about my sentiments? I have no particularly different story to tell you than what

그날 밤 일을 돌이키고 있었다. 어조에는 아직도 그날 밤의 심사가 조금도 실려 있질 않은 채였다.

"그래 저를 나무래서 냉큼 집안으로 데리고 들어갔더니라. 그리고 더운밥을 지어 먹여서 그 집에서 하룻밤을 재워 가지고 동도 트기 전에 길을 되돌려 떠나보냈더니라……."

"그래 그때 어머님 마음이 어떠셨어요."

"마음이 어떻기는야. 팔린 집이나마 거기서 하룻밤 저 아그를 재워 보내고 싶어 싫은 골목 드나들며 마당도 쓸고 걸레질도 훔치며 기다려 온 에미였는디, 더운밥 해 먹이고 하룻밤을 재우고 나니 그만만 해도 한 소원은 우선 풀린 것 같더구나."

"그래 어머님은 흡족한 기분으로 아들을 떠나보내셨다는 그런 말씀이시겠군요. 하지만 정말로 그게 그렇게 될 수가 있었을까요? 어머님은 정말로 그렇게 흡족한 마음으로 아들을 떠나보내실 수 있으셨을까 말씀이에요. 아들은 다시 학교로 돌아가는 길이었다 하더라도 어머님 자신은 그때 변변한 거처 하나 마련해 두시질 못하셨을 처지에 말씀이에요."

"나더러 또 무슨 이야길 더 하라는 것이냐."

"그때 아들을 떠나보내실 때 어머님 심경을 듣고 싶어요.

눈길 95

you've already been told. I sold the house by necessity, not by choice. Under the circumstances, it was the only way. Although I had to do it, I couldn't entirely forget the house. My son was hesitant about whether he should go into the house when I found him."

Unable to bear my wife's insistence, my mother finally spoke, but reluctantly, reminiscing about that last night in our old house. Her tone of voice carried none of her feelings on that distant night, however.

"I scolded him for being so timid around his own house and then took him inside immediately. I prepared a hot meal for him and had him spend the night there. Before dawn, I sent him back," my mother continued.

"How did you feel, Mother?"

"Well," my mother went on, "I wanted to have him spend the night in the house even if it was

객지 공부 가는 어린 아들을 그런 식으로 떠나보내시면서 어머님 자신도 거처가 없이 떠도셔야 했던 그때 처지에서 어머님이 겪으신 심경을 말씀예요."

"그만두거라. 다 쓸데없는 노릇이니라. 이야기를 한들 그때 마음이야 네가 어찌 다 알아들을 수가 있겠냐."

노인은 다시 이야기를 사양했다.

그러나 그 체념기가 완연한 노인의 어조에는 아직도 혼자 당신의 맘속으로만 지녀 온 어떤 이야기가 남아 있을 것 같았다.

나는 이제 더 이상 기다리고 있을 수가 없었다. 아내는 그런 나의 기미를 눈치 채고 있었다 하더라도 노인만은 아직 그걸 알지 못하고 있었다. 노인의 말을 그쯤에서 그만 중단시켜야 했다. 아내가 어떻게 나온다 하더라도 내게까지 그것을 알게 하고 싶지는 않을 노인이었다. 내 앞에선 더 이상 노인의 이야기가 계속될 수가 없었다.

나는 이윽고 헛기침을 한 번 하고서 그 노인의 눈길이 닿고 있는 장지문 앞으로 모습을 불쑥 드러내고 나섰다.

눈길 97

already sold. My desire to have him do so was so powerful that I swept the courtyard and mopped the floor while coming and going back and forth to the road, waiting for him to come. I felt great relief when I fulfilled my wish to offer him a hot meal and a warm bed. It brought me great happiness."

"So you sent your son off in a satisfied mood, then. But were you really happy to send him off like that? Were you truly pleased, Mother? What I'm trying to say is, your son had a place to which he could go back—his school. But what about you? You had no decent place to go."

"What are you trying to get at?" my mother asked sheepishly.

"I want to know how you genuinely felt when you sent your young son off to a school in a strange town the way you did, without having any place to go yourself. I just want to know how you truly felt. That's all."

"It doesn't matter. You might as well forget the idea. Even if I tell you, how can you possibly understand how I really felt then?"

My mother then became reticent because, I suspected, the story had been buried deep inside her heart for such a long time. I found myself impatient, though, not being able to wait any longer.

I had to intervene right then and there to stop my mother from talking. Even if my wife aggressively insisted upon having her way, I knew my mother well and knew she would not want me to find out about that night. If I were present, I knew the conversation between them could not continue, especially on my mother's part.

I made a dry coughing sound and presented myself abruptly in front of the sliding lattice door,

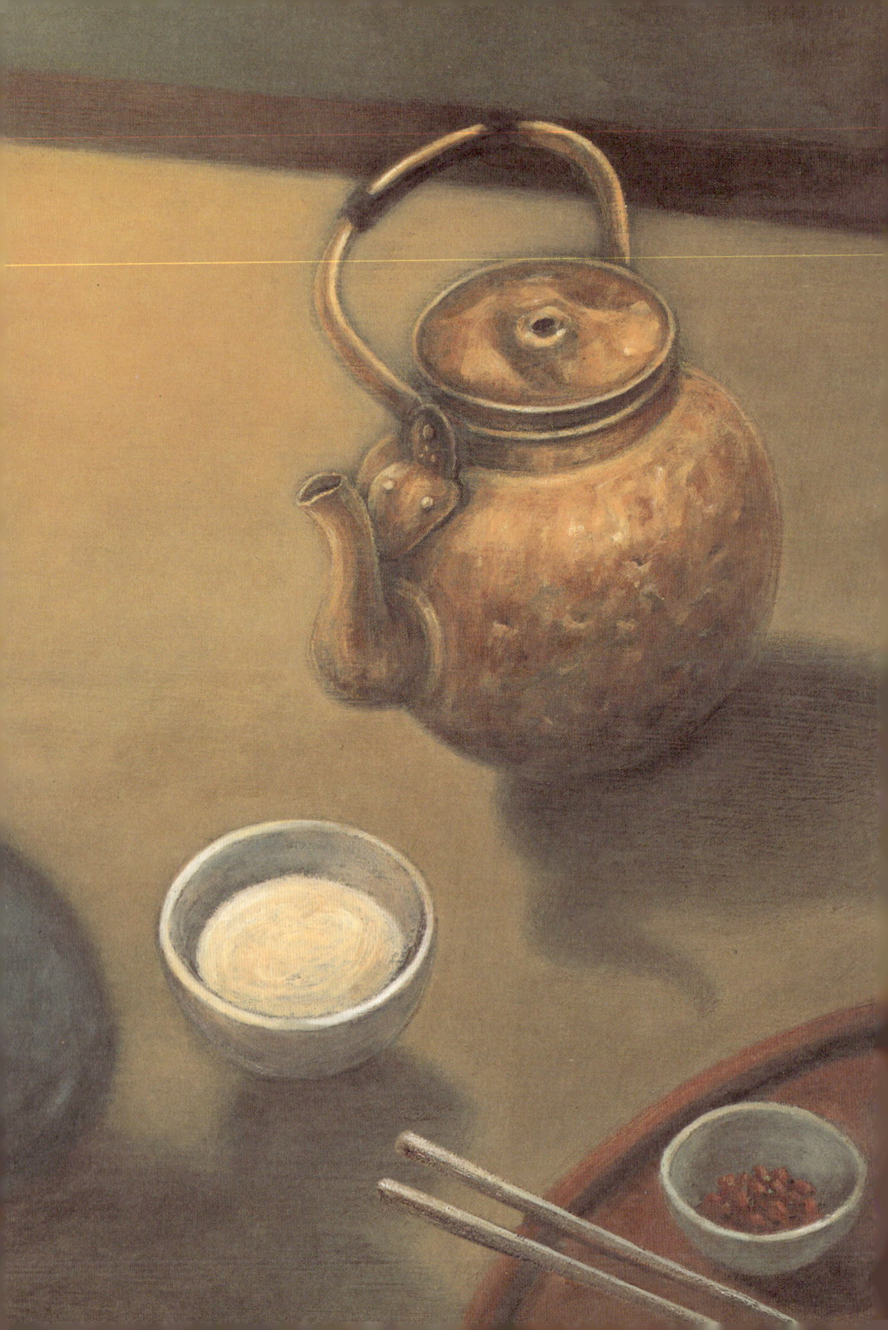

4

위험한 고비는 그럭저럭 모두 지나가고 있었다.

저녁상을 들일 때 노인은 또 언제나처럼 막걸리 한 되를 가져오게 하였다. 형의 술버릇 때문에 집안 꼴이 그 지경이 되었는데도 노인은 웬일로 내게 술 걱정을 그리 하지 않았다. 집에만 가면 당신이 손수 막걸리 한두 되씩을 꼭꼭 미리 마련해다 주곤 하였다.

한잔 마시고 잠이나 자거라.

그러면서 언제나 잠을 자기를 권하는 것이었다.

이날 저녁도 마찬가지였다.

"그래, 정 내일 아침으로 길을 나설라냐?"

저녁상이 들어왔을 때 노인은 그렇게 조심스런 목소리로 나의 내심을 한 번 더 떠 왔을 뿐이었다.

"가야 할 일이 있으니까 가겠다는 거 아니겠어요."

나는 노인에게 공연히 화가 치민 목소리로 퉁명스럽게 대꾸했다.

하니까 노인은 그것으로 그만이었다.

"그래 알았다. 저녁하고 술이나 한잔 하고 일찍 쉬거라."

on which my mother's eyes were fixed.

4

The danger seemed to pass. When supper was served, I was given a special bottle of rice wine by my mother, as she had always done for me. For some reason, she did not appear to be a bit concerned about my drinking, in spite of my late brother's abusive drinking habit, which eventually destroyed our family. Whenever I visited my mother, without fail, she bought a gallon of rice wine and then served it with her own hands.

"Have a glass of rice wine and go to sleep." In that way my mother always offered me a drink and wished me a good night's sleep afterwards. She did exactly the same thing on that evening.

"Do you really have to leave tomorrow

morning?" my mother asked carefully as we sat around the dinner table, trying to discern my real intentions.

"Yes, I have to go and take care of a few things," I replied bluntly, in an unnecessarily angry tone of voice. At my response, my mother became totally resigned to my decision.

"I understand. Why don't you have some rice wine with your meal and retire early, then?" Without uttering a single word, I obeyed her. I emptied nearly a half-gallon of the rice wine with my supper. And, as if I could not overcome the influence of the alcohol, I went to bed quite early. After my sister-in-law and her children left to find a place to sleep elsewhere, my mother, my wife, and I lay down in the room again as we had the previous night.

I felt I had managed to have those nearly critical hours come to an end. I shut my eyes and knew

아침부터 먼 길을 나서려면 잠이라도 일찍 자 두라는 것이었다. 나는 말없이 노인을 따랐다. 저녁 겸해서 술 한 되를 비우고 그리고 술기를 못 견디는 사람처럼 일찌감치 잠자리를 펴고 누웠다.

형수님이 조카들을 데리고 잠자리를 찾아 나가자 이날 밤도 우리는 세 사람 합숙이었다.

어쨌거나 이제 위태로운 고비는 그럭저럭 거의 다 넘겨 가고 있는 셈이었다. 눈을 붙였다. 깨고 나면 그것으로 모든 건 끝나는 것이었다. 지붕이고 옷궤고 더 이상 신경을 쓸 일이 없어진다. 노인에게 숨겨진 빚문서가 있을까. 하지만 이날 밤만 무사히 넘기고 나면 노인의 빚문서도 그것으로 영영 휴지가 되는 것이다.

—잠이나 자자. 빚이고 뭐고 잠들면 그만이다. 노인에게 빚은 내가 무슨 빚이 있단 말인가……

나는 제법 홀가분한 기분으로 눈을 감고 잠을 청했다. 술기 탓인지 알알한 잠 기운이 이내 눈꺼풀을 덮어 왔다.

한데 얼마쯤 그렇게 아늑한 졸음기 속을 헤매고 났을 때였을까. 나는 웬일인지 문득 다시 잠기가 서서히 엷어져 가고 있었다. 그리고 아직도 그 어렴풋한 선잠기 속에 도란도

that once I awoke the next morning, the visit would come to an end as I wished. I did not need to worry about the roof business, the dresser, or anything else for that matter. I wondered whether or not my mother had a hidden bill waiting in lie for me.

I'll try to go to sleep. Debt or not, everything will be all right once I fall asleep. How could I owe her anything, anyway? I kept telling myself this, trying to invite sleep to come to me. I was in quite a free and easy spirit. It must have been the rice wine because heavy drowsiness swept over me immediately, closing my eyelids.

I wandered in and out of a hazy sleep for some time before my drowsiness slowly lifted from me. I had no idea what had driven my sleepiness away. Even in my light sleep, I could vaguely hear my mother murmuring softly.

"On that night, we had a sudden, unusually

란 조심스런 노인의 말소리가 들려오고 있었다.

"그날 밤사말로 갑자기 웬 눈이 그리도 많이 내렸던지 잠을 잤으면 얼마나 잤겠느냐마는 그래도 잠시 눈을 붙였다가 새벽녘에 일어나 보니 바깥이 왼통 환한 눈 천지더구나……눈이 왔더라도 어쩔 수가 있더냐. 서둘러 밥 한술씩을 끓여다가 속을 덥히고 그 눈길을 서둘러 나섰더니라……"

나는 다시 정신이 번쩍 들고 말았다. 어찌된 일인지 노인이 마침내 그날 밤 이야기를 아내에게 가닥가닥 털어놓고 있는 중이었다.

"처지가 떳떳했으면 날이라도 좀 밝은 다음에 길을 나설 수도 있었으련만, 그땐 아직도 그리 처지가 부끄럽고 저주스럽기만 했던지……그래 할 수 없이 새벽 눈길을 둘이서 나섰지만, 시오리나 되는 장터 차부까지 산길이 멀기는 또 얼마나 멀더냐."

기억을 차근차근 더듬어 나가고 있는 노인의 몽롱한 목소리는 마치 어린 손주아이에게 옛 얘기라도 들려주고 있는 할머니의 그것처럼 아늑한 느낌마저 깃들고 있었다.

아내가 결국은 노인을 거기까지 유도해 냈음이 분명하였다.

"이야기를 한들 네가 어찌 다 알아들을 수가 있겠

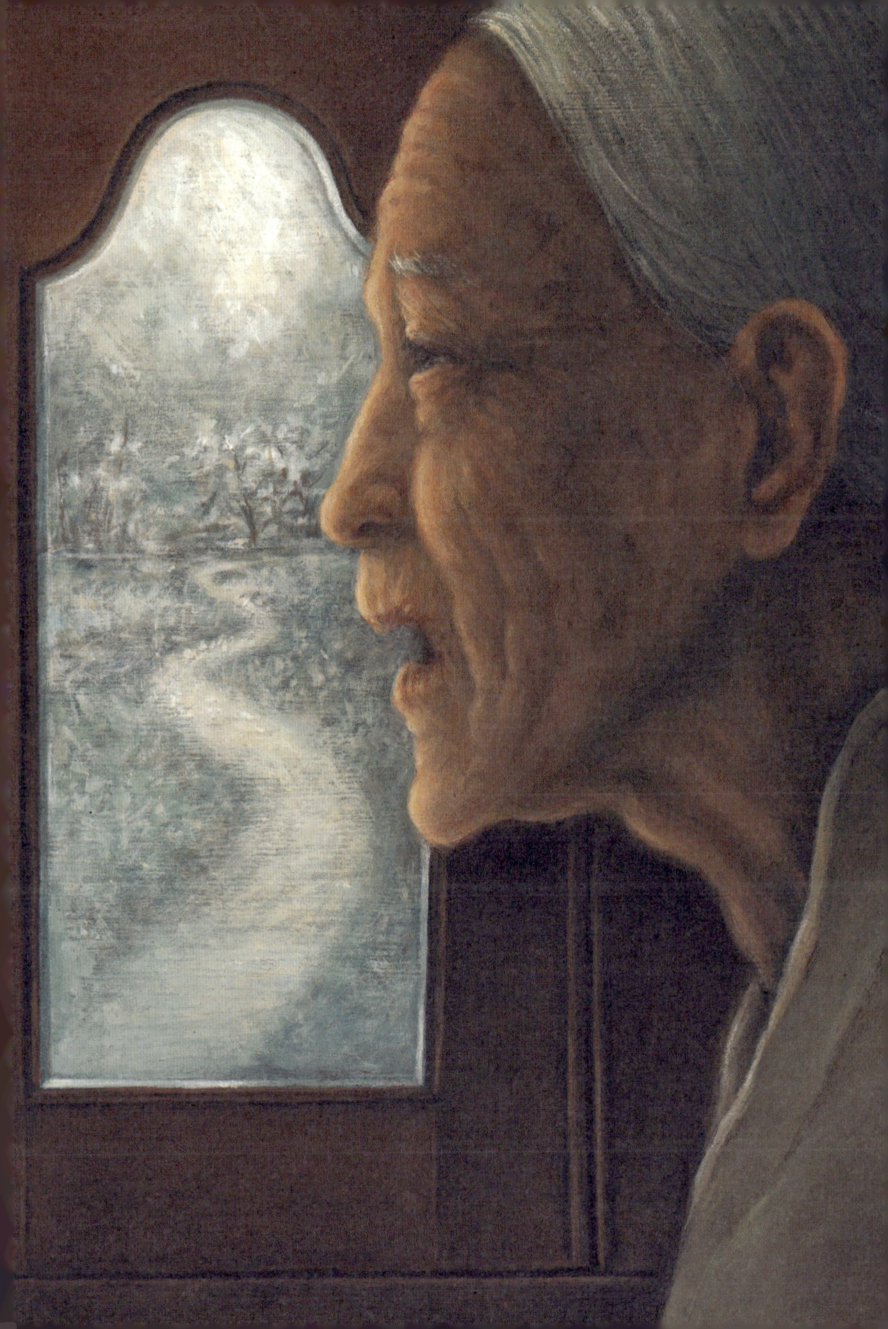

heavy snow fall," my mother was saying. "I tried to sleep, but could not. I only managed to sleep a few hours that night. When I woke up around daybreak, the entire world seemed to be covered with brilliant snow, but that didn't stop me. I busied myself with fixing breakfast, which warmed us. As soon as we finished our meal, we left in a hurry on a snow-covered road."

Suddenly, my mind became quite clear. It was beyond my belief that my mother was in the midst of finally disclosing to my wife the story of that night in our old house.

"Under normal circumstances, we could have left after sunrise," my mother continued. "I was still ashamed of my situation. I cursed my fate. However, I had no choice, so before dawn, my son and I were on the snowy road. It was nearly fifteen miles to the marketplace in town. It was a long, long walk along the mountain road."

My mother was revealing that day moment by moment. She talked gently, as if she were speaking to a little grandchild about an old tale. The way she talked gave me the sensation of snuggling up in bed to hear a grandparent's story, much like a child would do. My wife had finally succeeded in leading my mother to disclose her innermost thoughts.

"Even if I tell you, how can you possibly comprehend how I felt?" My mother paused before she resumed. "It was still dark. We slid and fell as we walked on the rough, slippery mountain road. However, we managed to arrive at the bus station on time." My mother was telling my wife about the night, no, the dawn, when she had accompanied me to the bus station. I had never, even once, told my wife about this particular event. I had desperately wanted to forget about that snowy road, wishing it would somehow disappear from my memory.

To my dismay, my mother was now going back to the past in her subdued voice, like she were mentioning an old debt that could never be repaid in any way. As I listened to my mother, the events of that day finally unfolded their wings in my head so clearly that I could touch them. Was my mother overwhelmed by her sense of sorrow for me? She had no alternative but to carry out what she had to do under the circumstances.

At first, she offered to accompany me only to where I would leave the village. Then she insisted upon accompanying me onto the side road that led from the village to the mountain. Even after we climbed the mountain pass, she insisted that we walk the path together until the newly constructed road appeared. Whenever she insisted upon accompanying me a longer distance, we ended up having an argument.

냐······."

 낮결에 노인이 말꼬리를 한 가닥 깔고 넘은 기미를 아내가 무심히 들어 넘겼을 리 없었다.

 그날 밤—아니 그날 새벽—아내에겐 한 번도 들려 준 일이 없는 그날 새벽의 서글픈 동행을, 나 자신도 한사코 기억의 피안으로 사라져 가 주기를 바라 오던 그 새벽의 눈길의 기억을 노인은 이제 받아 낼 길이 없는 묵은 빚문서를 들추듯 허무한 목소리로 되씹고 있었다.

 "날은 아직 어둡고 산길은 험하고, 미끄러지고 넘어지면서도 차부까지는 그래도 어떻게 시간을 대어 갈 수가 있었구나······."

 이야기를 듣고 있는 나의 머릿속에도 마침내 그날의 정경이 손에 닿을 듯 역력히 떠올랐다. 어린 자식놈의 처지가 너무도 딱해서였을까. 아니 어쩌면 노인 자신의 처지까지도 그밖엔 달리 도리가 없었을 노릇이었는지도 모른다. 동구 밖까지만 바래다주겠다던 노인은 다시 마을 뒷산의 잿길까지만 나를 좀 더 바래주마 우겼고, 그 잿길을 올라선 다음에는 새 신작로가 나설 때까지만 산길을 함께 넘어 가자 우겼다. 그럴 때마다 한 차례씩 가벼운 실랑이를 치르고 나면 노

눈길

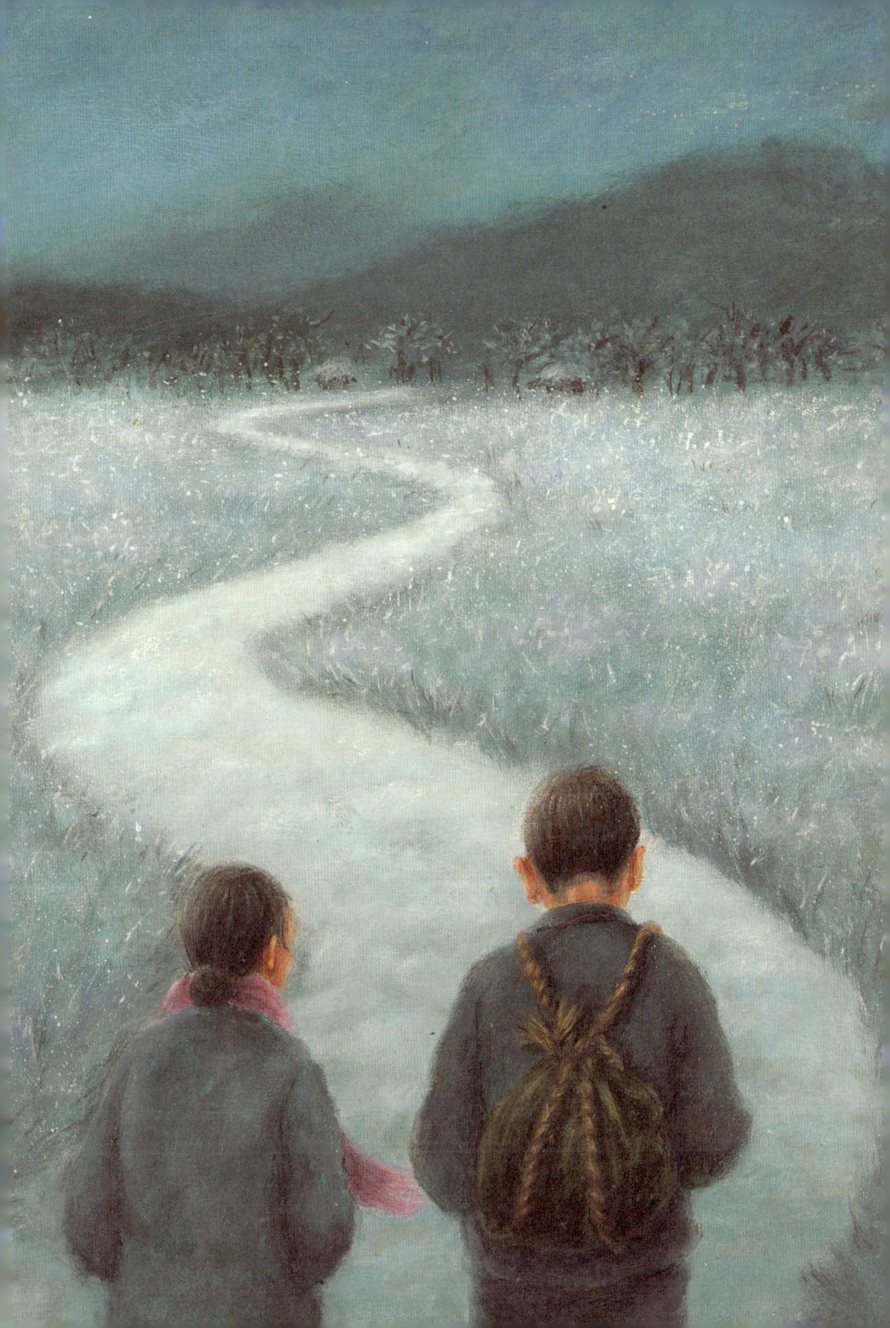

Except for these slight altercations, we said nothing to each other.

It would have been better if we had left the village after the sun had risen. Yet neither of us dared to leave after daybreak. All things considered, we found it preferable to leave the village before the veil of darkness lifted.

As my mother had mentioned to my wife previously, we walked, slid, and fell often on that snowy road. When I fell, my mother would help me get up and vice versa. In this manner, we emerged on the main road in silence. Even from that point, a considerable distance remained before we reached the bus station near the town office. My mother and I ended up walking along the main road all the way to the terminal. It was still not daybreak.

I do not recall what happened to us after that. I got on the bus and saw my mother walking back

인과 나는 더 이상 할 말이 있을 수가 없었다. 아닌게 아니라 날이라도 좀 밝은 다음이었으면 좋았겠는데 날이 밝기를 기다려 동네를 나서는 건 노인이나 나나 생각을 않았다. 그나마 그 어둠을 타고 마을을 나서는 것이 노인이나 나나 마음이 편했다. 노인의 말마따나 미끄러지고 넘어지면서, 내가 미끄러지면 노인이 나를 부축해 일으키고, 노인이 넘어지면 내가 당신을 부축해 가면서, 그렇게 말없이 신작로까지 나섰다. 그러고도 아직 그 면소 차부까지는 길이 한참이나 남아 있었다. 나는 결국 그 면소 차부까지도 노인과 함께 신작로를 걸었다.

아직도 날이 밝기 전이었다.

하지만 그러고 우리는 어찌 되었던가.

나는 차를 타고 떠나가 버렸고, 노인은 다시 그 어둠 속의 눈길을 되돌아선 것이다.

내가 알고 있는 건 거기까지 뿐이었다.

노인이 그 후 어떻게 길을 되돌아갔는지는 나로서도 아직 들은 바가 없었다. 노인을 길가에 혼자 남겨 두고 차로 올라서 버린 그 순간부터 나는 차마 그 노인을 생각하기가 싫었고, 노인도 오늘까지 그날의 뒷 얘기는 들려준 일이 없었다.

눈길 115

to the village along the snowy road in darkness. That was everything I remembered. My memory stopped right there. I had never been told how my mother managed to return to the village after she saw me off at the bus station. From the moment l got on the bus, leaving my mother all alone, I did not want to think of her. She had never uttered a single word to me about what happened to her after that early dawn.

Today, for some reason, she was recalling every moment of that morning.

"After we managed to enter the streets of the marketplace, we hurried on until we saw the bus station in the distance. The bus was about to leave the garage and I had to wave my arms frantically to stop it. The bus driver barely stopped the bus, but he did let my son on. He disappeared from my sight, only leaving a clanking noise in his wake."

한데 노인은 웬일로 오늘사 그날의 기억을 끝까지 돌이키고 있었다.

"어떻게 어떻게 장터 거리로 들어서서 차부가 저만큼 보일 만한 데까지 가니까 그때 마침 차가 미리 불을 켜고 차부를 나오는구나. 급한 김에 내가 손을 휘저어 그 차를 세웠더니, 그래 그 운전수란 사람들은 어찌 그리 길이 급하고 매정하기만 한 사람들이더냐. 차를 미처 세우지도 덜하고 덜크렁 덜크렁 눈 깜짝할 사이에 저 아그를 훌쩍 실어 담고 가 버리는구나."

"그래서 어머님은 그때 어떻게 하셨어요?"

잠잠히 입을 다문 채 듣고만 있던 아내가 모처럼 한마디를 끼어들고 있었다.

나는 갑자기 다시 노인의 이야기가 두려워지고 있었다. 자리를 차고 일어나 다음 이야기를 가로막고 싶었다. 하지만 나는 이미 그럴 수가 없었다. 사지가 말을 들어 주지 않았다. 온몸이 마치 물을 먹은 솜처럼 무겁게 가라앉아 있었다. 몸을 어떻게 움직여 볼 수가 없었다. 형언하기 어려운 어떤 달콤한 슬픔, 달콤한 피곤기 같은 것이 나를 아늑히 감싸 오고 있었다.

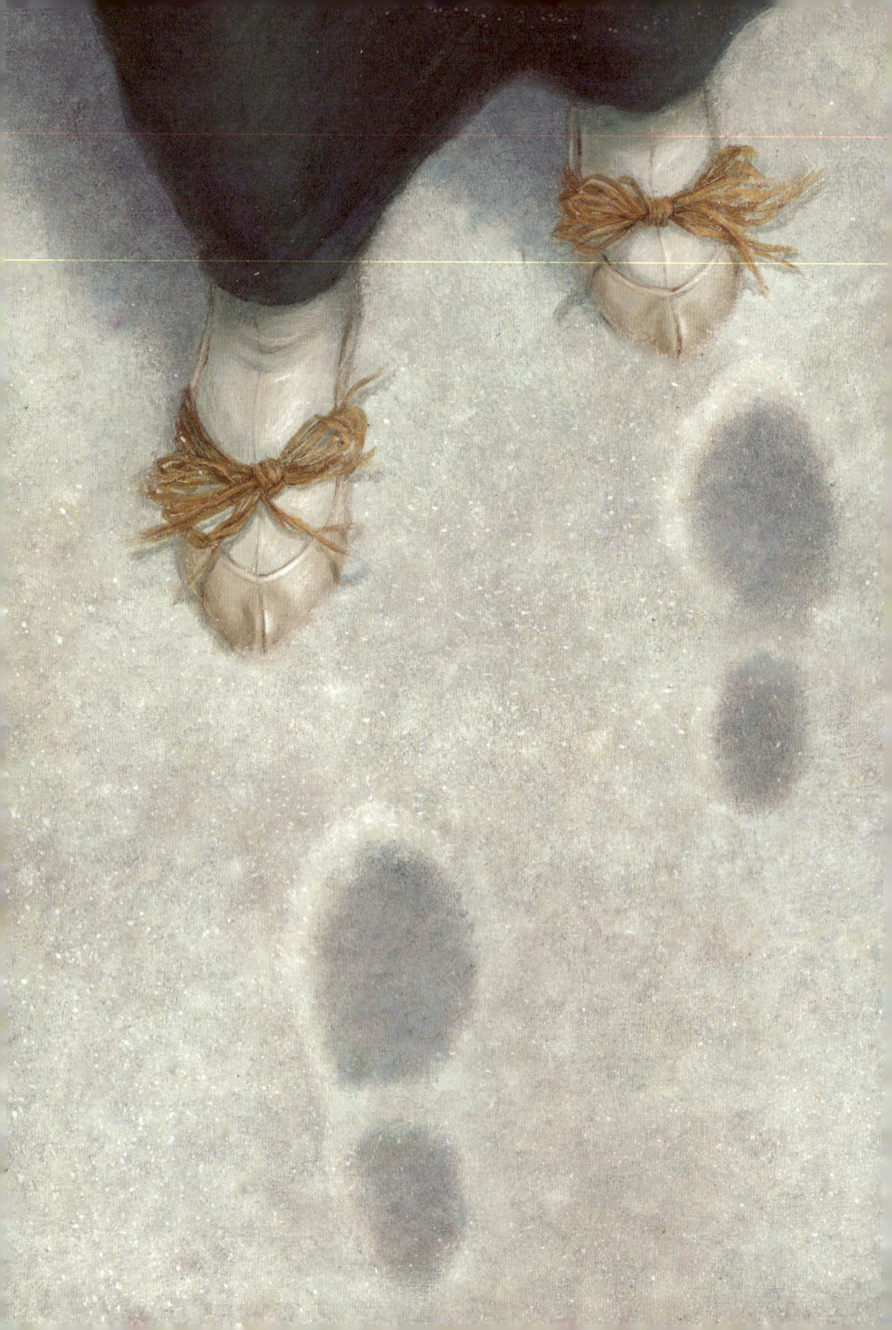

"어떻게 하기는야. 넋이 나간 사람마냥 어둠 속에서 한참이나 찻길만 바라보고 서 있을 수밖에야……그 허망한 마음을 어떻게 다 말 할 수가 있을 거나……."

노인은 여전히 옛 얘기를 하듯 하는 그 차분하고 아득한 음성으로 그날의 기억을 더듬어 나갔다.

"한참 그러고 서 있다 보니 찬바람에 정신이 좀 되돌아오더구나. 정신이 들어 보니 갈 길이 새삼 허망스럽지 않았겠냐. 지금까진 그래도 저하고 나하고 둘이서 함께 헤쳐 온 길인데 이참에는 그 길을 늙은 것 혼자서 되돌아서려니……거기다 아직도 날은 어둡지야……그대로는 암만해도 길을 되돌아설 수가 없어 차부를 찾아 들어갔더니라. 한식경이나 차부 안 나무 걸상에 웅크리고 앉아 있으려니 그제사 동녘 하늘이 훤해져 오더구나……그래서 또 혼자 서두를 것도 없는 길을 서둘러 나섰는데, 그때 일만은 언제까지도 잊혀질 수가 없을 것 같구나."

"길을 혼자 돌아가시던 그때 일을 말씀이세요?"

"눈길을 혼자 돌아가다 보니 그 길엔 아직도 우리 둘 말고는 아무도 지나간 사람이 없지 않았겠냐. 눈발이 그친 그 신작로 눈 위에 저하고 나하고 둘이 걸어온 발자국만 나란히

"So what did you do afterwards, Mother?"

Suddenly, I was afraid of my mother continuing her tale. I was tempted to get up from my bedding and prevent her from talking any further. Even though the possibility existed in my mind, my limbs wouldn't cooperate. My whole body sank into the depths of the sea, making me feel heavy as if I were waterlogged cotton. I could not move my body in any direction. The sense of a certain sweet sorrow, or sweet fatigue, that was beyond description, hazily embraced me.

"What do you think I did? Like a person who has lost her senses, I stood still in the darkness by the roadside for a good while, staring at the point in the road where the bus disappeared. How can I put it into proper words how empty I felt then?" My mother continued speaking calmly in her controlled tone of voice, as if she were reminiscing about a past from which she was emotionally far removed.

"I don't know how long I stood there like that," my mother continued. "My senses came back somewhat as the cold wind licked my face. When I thought of returning to the village, I was gripped with a new sense of emptiness. Before he left, he and I had walked along the rough road together. When I was reminded that I, an old woman, had to go back alone, I couldn't make myself return. To make matters worse, it was still dark, so I went inside the bus station and sat down on a wooden chair, resting my forehead on my knees. After nearly an hour, the eastern sky began to lighten. Even though I didn't have to make haste, I started to walk back hurriedly. I don't think I'll ever forget that early morning as long as I live."

"You mean the time when you had to go back to the village alone?"

"As I walked alone along the same snowy road

we had walked on before, not one footprint was on it besides our own. Not a single soul had passed by since then. I could still see our footprints, side by side, still distinctively imprinted on the newly-built road where the snowfall had stopped."

"You must have missed him very much when you were looking at his footprints, Mother," my wife commented thoughtfully.

"I did, my dear. I missed him very much; more than I can describe. I passed by the end of the main road and set foot on the winding mountain road. Even then I could see his footprints. I felt both his warm body and his friendly voice in them. Whenever wild pigeons flew by noisily, I wondered if my son's soul was returning to me as a pigeon. I was also confused when I looked at the snow-clad trees, like he would appear anytime from behind them. As I was walking in

이어져 있구나."

"그래서 어머님은 그 발자국 때문에 아들 생각이 더 간절하셨겠네요."

"간절하다 뿐이었겠냐. 신작로를 지나고 산길을 들어서도 굽이굽이 돌아온 그 몹쓸 발자국들에 아직도 도란도란 저 아그의 목소리나 따뜻한 온기가 남아 있는 듯만 싶었제. 산비둘기만 푸르륵 날아가도 저 아그 넋이 새가 되어 다시 되돌아오는 듯 놀라지고, 나무들이 눈을 쓰고 서 있는 것만 보아도 뒤에서 금세 저 아그 모습이 뛰어나올 것만 싶었지야. 하다 보니 나는 굽이굽이 외지기만 한 그 산길을 저 아그 발자국만 따라 밟고 왔더니라. 내 자석아, 내 자석아, 너하고 나하고 둘이 온 길을 이제는 이 몹쓸 늙은 것 혼자서 너를 보내고 돌아가고 있구나!"

"어머님 그때 우시지 않았어요?"

"울기만 했겠냐. 오목 오목 디뎌 논 그 아그 발자국마다 한도 없는 눈물을 뿌리며 돌아왔제. 내 자석아, 부디 몸이나 성하게 지내거라. 부디 부디 너라도 좋은 운 타서 복 받고 살거라……눈앞이 가리도록 눈물을 떨구면서 눈물로 저 아그 앞길을 빌고 왔제……."

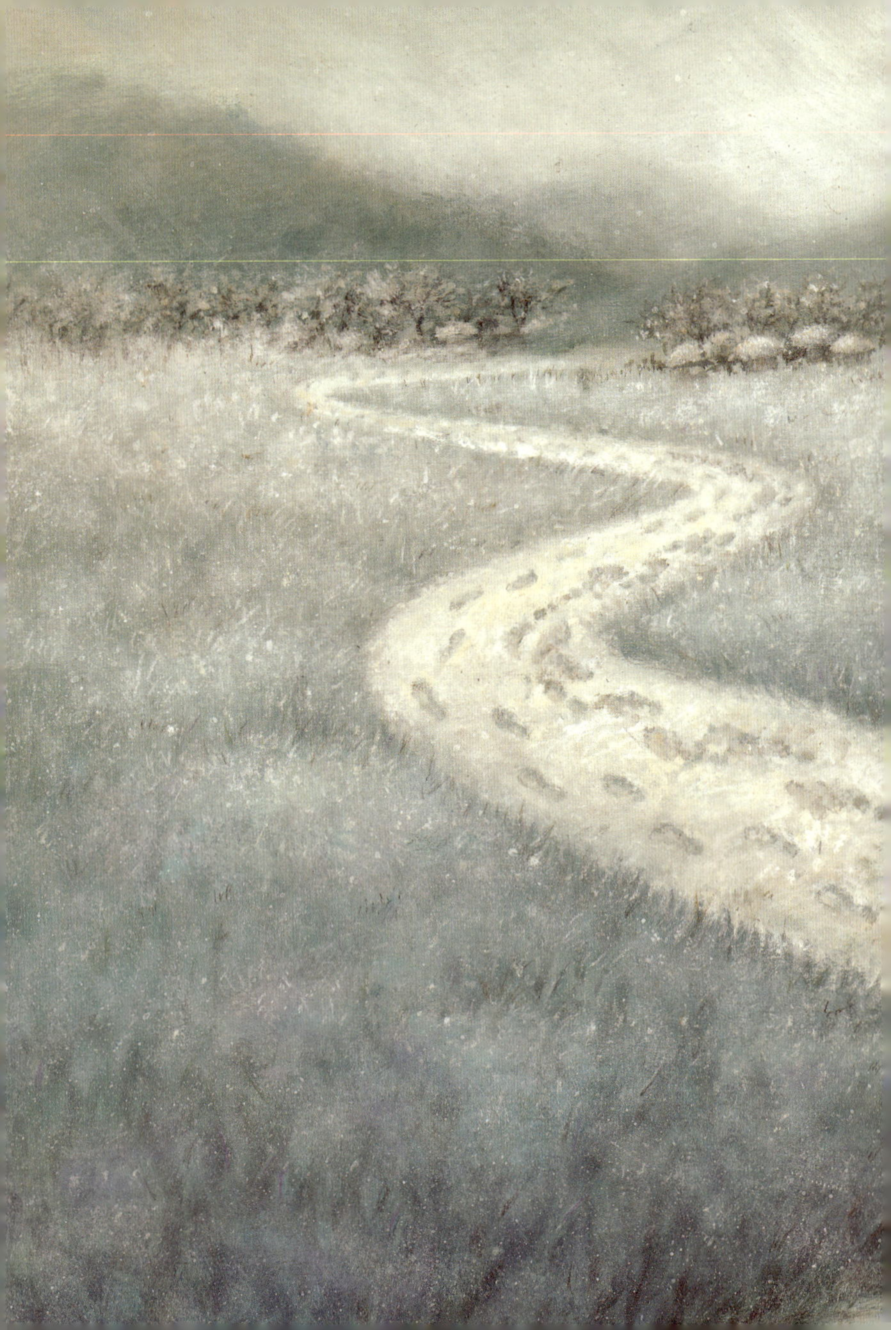

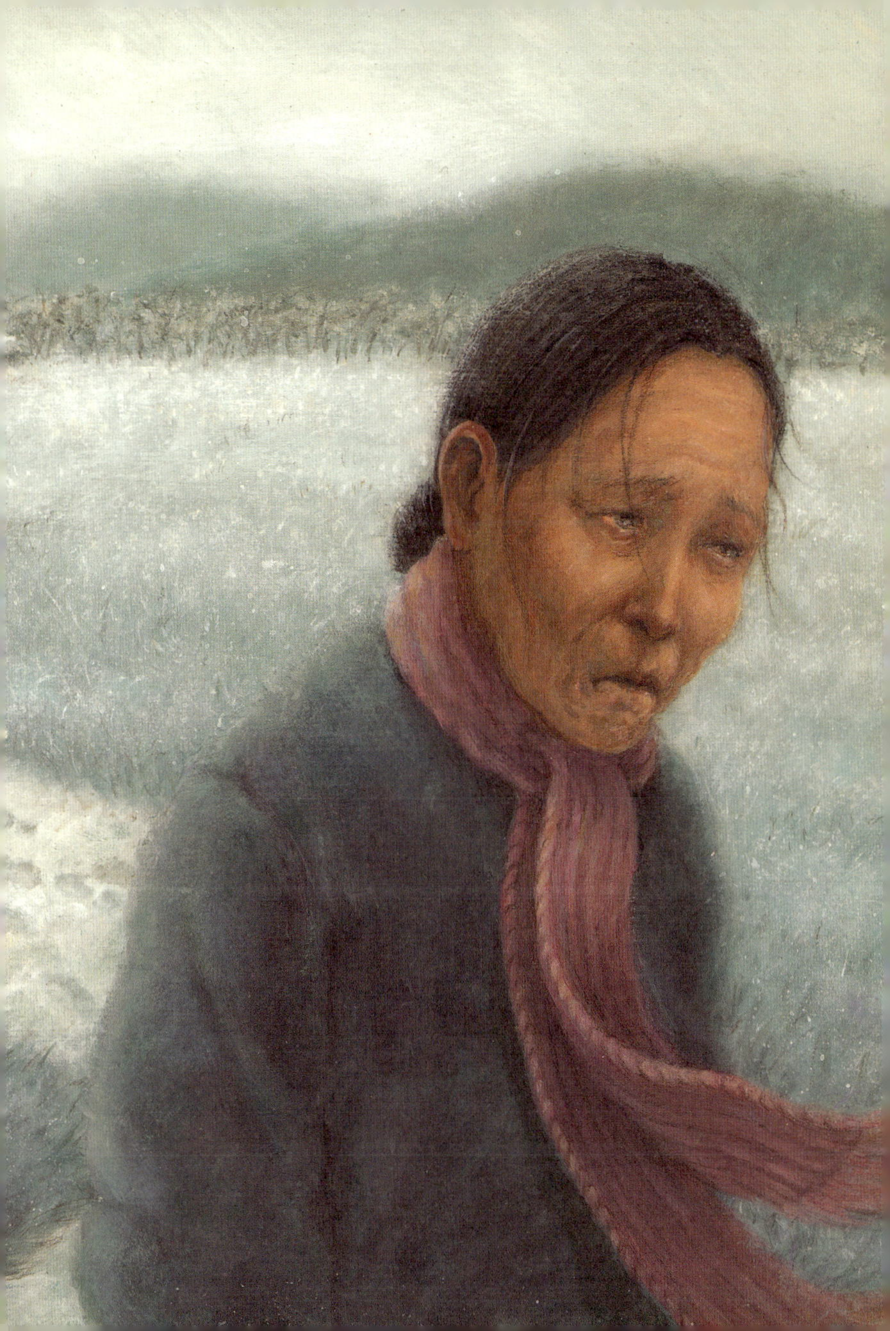

that frame of mind, along the winding, lonesome mountain road, I only followed his footprints in the snow. 'Oh, my son, my son—now I, this wretched old woman, am returning all alone after sending you off, taking this same road you and I walked together,' I said to myself."

"Were you crying?"

"Yes, I was. I did more than cry. I wept ceaselessly over his vivid footprints. I wept for his every step. I wished him the very best, calling to him, 'Oh my son, my son, please stay healthy. Please live a good, comfortable life. I hope you'll receive many blessings even if only you are left among our family.' I prayed for his promising future in my tears and wept until my eyes blurred."

My mother's story seemed to be nearly over now. My wife was speechless.

"Anyhow, although I took a good long time

노인의 이야기는 이제 거의 끝이 나 가고 있는 것 같았다. 아내는 이제 할 말을 잊은 듯 입을 조용히 다물고 있었다.

 "그런디 그 서두를 것도 없는 길이라 그렁그렁 시름없이 걸어온 발걸음이 그래도 어느 참에 동네 뒷산을 당도해 있었구나. 하지만 나는 그 길로는 차마 동네를 바로 들어설 수가 없어 잿등 위에 눈을 쓸고 아직도 한참이나 시간을 기다리고 앉아 있었더니라……."

 "어머님도 이젠 돌아가실 거처가 없으셨던 거지요."

 한동안 조용히 입을 다물고 있던 아내가 이제 더 이상 참을 수가 없어진 듯 갑자기 노인을 추궁하고 나섰다. 그녀의 목소리는 이제 울먹임 때문에 떨리고 있었다.

 나 역시도 이젠 더 이상 노인을 참을 수가 없었다. 이제나마 노인을 가로막고 싶었다. 아내의 추궁에 대한 그 노인의 대꾸가 너무도 두려웠다. 노인의 대답을 들을 수가 없었다. 하지만 그 역시도 불가능한 일이었다.

 나는 아직도 눈을 뜰 수가 없었다. 불빛 아래 눈을 뜨고 일어날 수가 없었다. 사지가 마비된 듯 가라앉아 있는 때문만이 아니었다. 졸음기가 아직 아쉬워서도 아니었다. 눈꺼풀 밑으로 뜨겁게 차 오르는 것을 아내와 노인 앞에 보일 수

눈길 127

walking around aimlessly, I managed to reach the mountainside behind the village. As I had no reason to make haste, I couldn't bring myself to enter the village immediately. So I cleared the snow from a place on the path and sat there for a long while."

"You didn't have any place to go back to then, did you, Mother?"

My wife, who had remained silent for some time, asked this as if she were unable to keep her silence any longer. Her tearful tone of voice was now trembling with emotion. I, likewise, could not endure my mother's story any longer. I wanted to intervene. I was exceedingly troubled about her response to my wife's question. I could not bear listening to her reply, although I knew well it was impossible for me to avoid it. I was still unable to open my eyes, however. I simply could not open them under the light, or get up. It

가 없었다. 그것이 너무도 부끄러웠기 때문이었다. 아내는 이번에도 그러는 나를 알고 있었던 것 같았다.

"여보, 이젠 좀 일어나 보세요. 일어나서 당신도 말을 좀 해 보세요."

그녀가 느닷없이 나를 세차게 흔들어 깨웠다. 그녀의 음성은 이제 거의 울부짖음에 가까왔다. 그래도 나는 일어날 수가 없었다. 뜨거운 것을 숨기기 위해 눈꺼풀을 꾹꾹 눌러 참으면서 내처 잠이 든 척 버틸 수밖에 없었다.

음성이 아직 흐트러지지 않고 있는 건 오히려 그 노인뿐이었다.

"그만 두거라. 아침 길 나서기도 피곤할 것인디 곤하게 자고 있는 사람 뭣 하러 그러냐."

노인은 일단 아내의 행동을 말려 두고 나서 아직도 그 옛얘기를 하는 듯한 아득하고 차분한 음성으로 당신의 남은 이야기를 끝맺어 가고 있었다.

"그런디 이것만은 네가 잘못 안 것 같구나. 그때 내가 뒷산 잿등에서 동네를 바로 들어가지 못하고 있었던 일 말이다. 그건 내가 갈 데가 없어 그랬던 건 아니란다. 산 사람 목숨인데 설마 그때라고 누구네 문간방 한 칸에라도 산 몸뚱

was not just the sinking sensation that gave me total paralysis of my limbs, nor was it any lingering drowsiness that prevented me from getting up. The reason was that I could not show the warm tears that soaked my eyelids to my mother or my wife. I was too ashamed.

Abruptly my wife shook me with force, causing me to become wide awake. "Please get up, dear, and say something. Please!" she urged. It seemed she already knew of my emotion. The tone of her voice was pleading. Despite her efforts, I did not get up. I shut my eyes more tightly to hold back the surging tears. I pretended to sleep soundly.

"Let him be. Don't bother him. He's sleeping so soundly, and he needs the rest since he's leaving early tomorrow morning," my mother said calmly. She did not lose her self-control. "You're mistaken about one thing," she then concluded in her composed and somewhat nostalgic voice. It

이 깃들일 데 마련이 안됐겠냐. 갈 데가 없어서가 아니라 아침 햇살이 너무 눈에 시리더구나, 그때는 벌써 동네 아래까지 햇살이 활짝 퍼져 들어 있는디, 눈에 덮인 그 우리 집 지붕까지도 햇살 때문에 볼 수가 없더구나. 더구나 동네에선 아침 짓는 연기가 한참인디 그렇게 시린 눈을 해 갖고는 그 햇살이 부끄러워 차마 어떻게 동네 골목을 들어설 수가 있더냐. 그놈의 말간 햇살이 부끄러워져서 그럴 엄두가 안 생겨나더구나. 시린 눈이라도 좀 가라앉히자고 그래 그러고 앉아 있었더니라……."

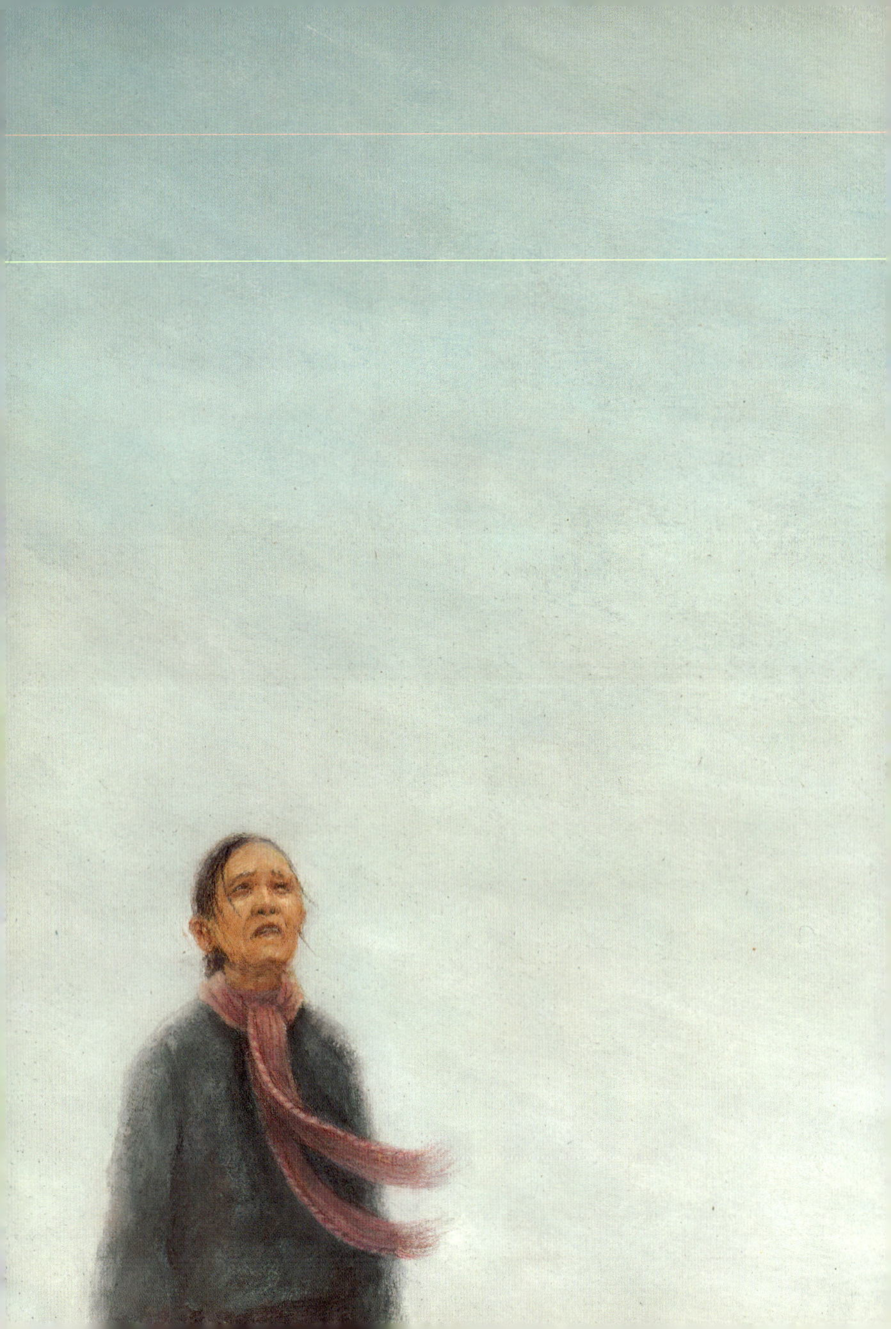

was like she was still talking about some old, half-forgotten tale. "The reason I couldn't leave the mountain passage and enter the village right away wasn't because I had no place to go once I got to the village. As long as I'm alive, I'll be capable of taking care of myself. You see, I had already managed to secure a small rented room for myself. It was the blinding sunlight of morning, not the uncertainty of finding a place to live; the whole village was showered with blissful sunlight. I couldn't even look at the snow-covered roof of our old house because of the sunlight. What's more is that all the chimneys throughout the village were smoking from fires of breakfasts being prepared. How could I dare walk into the village feeling so ashamed? I couldn't face direct sunlight in this frame of mind. The bright sunlight made me feel so awful that I couldn't even attempt to take one single step. I merely sat there, thoughtfully, hoping to adjust my eyes to the blinding rays of light...."

이청준 단편 소설 『눈길』 해설
On Yi Chong-jun's short story, *The Snowy Road*

어머니의 자식 사랑은 지극하다. 세상의 많은 어머니들은 자신의 모든 것을 희생하면서까지 자식을 보살핀다. 그러나 사랑하는 마음이 지극해도 사랑을 베풀지 못하는 경우가 있다. 가난이나 죽음이나 이별 그리고 전쟁과 같은 가혹한 상황 속에서 어쩔 수 없이 자식에 대한 사랑을 베풀지 못하는 어머니들이 있다. 그러한 어머니들의 가슴에는 한이 맺힌다. 『눈길』은 가난 때문에 사랑이 더 큰 고통이 되어 버린 어머니와 아들의 이야기이다.

20세기 중엽 한국의 시골 마을에 한 어머니가 있었다. 남편은 죽고, 결혼한 큰아들과 며느리와 함께 살고 있었다. 작은 아들은 도회에서 고등학교에 다니고 있었다. 큰아들이 술중독자가 되어 재산을 탕진하고 죽자, 어머니는 집도 없는 가난뱅이 신세가 된다. 이제 둘째 아들이 고향에 돌아와도 머물 집이 없다. 어린 자식에게 고향이란 어머니와 고향집이 있는 곳이다. 그러나 이제 어머니는 어린 자식의 뒤를 보살펴 줄 능력이 없고, 고향집은 팔려 버렸다. 어머니는 주체 못 할 고통과 절망 속에서도 둘째 아들을 생각한다. 마지막으로 둘째 아들을 고향집에서 재우고 따뜻한 밥을 해 먹이며 어머니로서의 사랑을 베풀고자 한다. 그래서 어머니는 새집주인에게 부탁을 해서 둘째 아들이 올 때까지만 그 집에서 머물게 해달라고 부탁한다. 어머니는 이미 남의 소유가 된 집에 머물면서 날마다 둘째 아들이 오기를 기다린다. 마침내 둘째 아들이 소식을 듣고 고향으로 돌아온다. 어머니는 따뜻한 밥을 지어서 아들에게 먹이고, 잠자리를 마련해 준다. 그것은 고향집에서 어머니가 지어 주시는 마지막 밥이며, 어머니가 펴 주시는 마지막 잠자리이다.

이튿날 새벽, 어머니는 아들을 도회로 돌려보내야 한다. 도회로 나가는 차를 타려면, 읍내 차부까지 걸어가야 한다. 이제 아들은 도회로 나가면 혼자 힘으로 험한 세상을 버텨야 한다. 돌아올 고향집도 없고, 어머니는 더 이상 어린 아들의 뒤를 보살펴 줄 힘이 없다. 그렇게 아들을 떠나보내야 하는 어머니의 마음은 처절하다. 어머니는 차마 아들을 그냥 보내지 못하고 멀리까지 배웅한다. 처음에는 큰길까지 만 배웅해 주려 했지만, 결국 신작로를 걷고 고개를 지나서 읍내 차부까지 따라간다. 간밤에 내린 눈 때문에 길은 하얀 눈으로 덮여 있다. 어두운 새벽에 어머니와 아들은 눈길을 나란히 걷는다. 미끄러운 언덕에서는 서로를 의지하면 걷는다. 어머니도 아들도 눈물을 참으며, 하얀 눈 위에 나란히 발자국을 남긴다.

아들과 헤어지기 서러운 어머니의 마음이지만, 야속하게도 버스는 그들이 차부에 도착하자마자 아들을 싣고 떠나 버린다. 어머니는 텅 빈 차부에서 넋을 놓고 한참 앉았다가 이윽고 발길을 돌린다. 진짜 슬픔은 여기서부터 이다. 아직도 날은 밝지 않았다. 어머니는 하얀 눈길 위에 나란히 찍힌 두 사람의 발자국을 되짚으며 마을로 돌아간다. 어머니의 조그만 발은 아들의 체온이라도 느끼려는 듯이 아들이 남긴 발자국만 디디며 걷는다. 이제 어머니는 눈물을 감추지 않는다. 그 발자국에는 아들의 목소리나 온기가 남은 듯 했고, 산새가 푸드득 날아오르면 아들의 넋이 새가 된 듯이 놀라고, 나무들이 눈을 뒤집어 쓰고 있는 것을 보면 아들의 모습인 듯 했다. 눈길에는 두 사람의 발자국 외에 다른 흔적도 남았을 것이다. 되돌아오는 길에 어머니가 한없이 뿌린 눈물도 하얀 눈길 위에 상처 같은 흔적을 남겼을 것이기 때문이다. 그리고 눈이 녹으면서 눈길 위의 자국들은 없어졌겠지만, 어머니의 마음속에 남은 상처는 영원히 지워지지 않았을 것이다.

『눈길』은 한국 소설 가운데서 어머니의 사랑을 가장 애절하고 가장 감동적으로 보여 주는 작품이다.

A mother's love for her child is extreme devotion. Scores of mothers in the world take care of their children even if they must sacrifice everything they have. However, in some cases they are unable to express their love even though their love for them is bountiful. There are some mothers who are forced to ineffectively show their love due to harsh circumstances such as poverty, death, separation, and war. It is these same mothers whose hearts are heavy with regret. *The Snowy Road* is the story of a mother whose love for her son became fraught with distress due to her poverty.

The plot centers around a mother in a remote country village whose husband is dead. The mother lives with her oldest son—an alcoholic—and his wife, while her younger son attends high school in the city. When her alcoholic older son dies after squandering all the family's assets, she is left penniless and without a home. As a result, she has no home for her younger son when he comes to visit her.

To a young child, a hometown is a special place where one's mothe lives. In *the Snowy Road*, the mother finds herself being incapable of supporting her younger son because her house has been sold. Even when she is in a torrent of anguish and despair, she thinks only of her younger son. She yearns to show her maternal affection by fixing him a hot meal and making it possible for him to spend one last night with her in the house that's been sold, so she asks the new owner a favor, arranging for her to stay in the house until her son's visit. She stays on in the house, which has already been bought by someone else, waiting every day for her son's visit. Finally, her younger son returns to his hometown after he hears the news. She fixes a hot meal and prepares his bedding for him. It is the last hot meal she prepares and the last bedding she will ever lay out in the house.

The following day, at the break of dawn, the mother has to send her son back to the city. In order to catch a city-bound bus, one must walk all the way from the village to the bus terminal in town. Once her son returns to the city, he has to wrestle with the brutal world on his own. The mother has no house for her son to return to, and she no longer has any means to provide for him. Sending her son off in this way makes her heart tremendously heavy. She cannot find it in her to send him off this way, so she walks with him for some distance. At first, she intends to walk with him only up to the main road. However, she ends up walking with her son up to the newly constructed road, climbing over the crest of a hill and going all the way to the bus terminal. The road is blanketed with white snow that fell the previous night. The mother and her son walk side by side on the snowy road at the crack of dawn, supporting each other, as they leave their footprints in the snow. All the while the mother fights to hold back her tears.

Ignoring the mother who can't bear to part with her son, the indifferent bus driver speeds away, carrying her son away from the terminal. At a loss, she sits down in the empty terminal for a long while before eventually getting up to leave. The real grief begins at this point. The day has not yet broken. The mother returns to the village as she retraces the footprints left by her and her son on the snowy road. The mother's tiny feet only walk over her son's footprints, as if she wants to feel his bodily warmth from these imprints in the snow. At this point, she doesn't bother to hide her tears. She feels as if her son's voice and warm body temperature have been left in his footprints. While the mountain birds flutter above, she becomes dazed, as if her son's soul has become a bird. When she sees trees canopied by snow, she feels as though her son is among them; the mother believes there must be another trace of her son left behind besides his footprints. The endless tears that the mother has shed must also have left a trace, like a scar, on the snowy road on her way back to the village.

When the snow melts, the footprints on the snowy road will disappear. However, the lingering scar in the mother's heart will never heal. *The Snowy Road* is the most poignant and heartbreaking story of a mother's love expressed in Korean literature.

이남호 · 문학평론가, 고려대학교 교수
Lee Nam-ho · Literary Critic and Professor at Korea University

한국적 모성(母性)의 진면목을 표현하기 위한 노력
Striving to Express the True Nature of Korean Motherhood

1900년대 중반 하고도 60년대 초반은 족히 되어 보일, 전라도 하고도 깊고 깊은 산골이 분명한 소설 속의 시공간적 배경을, 도시에서 자란 그러고도 서울도 아닌 뉴욕에서 그림 공부를 한 최재은이 어떻게 소화해 낼 수 있을 것인가를 염려하지 않았던 것은 아니다. 하지만 기교 부리지 않는 사실적 표현을 통해 남도(南都)를 재현하기 위하여는, 또한 복선 속에 복선으로 도사리고 있는 한국적 모성의 진면목을 전달하기 위하여는, 본질을 향해 접근하고자 하는 최재은의 탁월한 묘사력이 절대적으로 필요했다고 본다.

그림 전체를 통해 깔려 있는 고지식한 구도와 색상은, '구질구질할 만큼 눈물겨운' 어머니의 모습이라고 해 두자. 그것은 극복할래야 극복할 수 없는 시대의 남루한 잔상을 정면으로 비난하거나 받아들이기에는 성성한 가슴으로는 도

무지 가능해 보이지 않는, 어머니를 둘러싼 남도식의 정서를 표현하기 위한 연출이었음을 염두에 두자.

하지만 최재은의 그림 속에 이와 같은 지리멸렬한 연출만이 있는 것은 아니다. 어머니의 가슴 속 '눈길'을 끌어내는 지점에서 옷궤에 달린 거울을 통로로 이용, 담담하게 현재와 과거를 연결해 주고 있는 부분에서는 새벽 칼바람 속을 가르는 눈발이 어느덧 책 속에 한 페이지 두 페이지 날리기 시작하고 있음을 경험할 수 있다. 눈 내리는 새벽길을 아들과 함께 걸을 때의 흐트러짐 없이 반듯하게 쪽져진 머리라던가, 눈길에 찍힌 두 사람의 발자국을 되짚어 돌아오는 발걸음을 클로즈업한 장면에 고무신을 동여맨 짚새기 매듭의 모습이라던가, 어머니 목에 감긴 목도리의 색상이 여린 분홍빛을 띠고 있다던가와 같은 서정은 나무등걸같이 거칠기만 한 어머니 손 안에 품은 여리고 따스한 사랑처럼 대조를 이루며 관객의 마음을 움직일 수 있으리라 본다.

마지막 장면 허망하고 막막하기만 한 새벽 하늘을 우러르는 그림 속 어머니 뺨에 눈물이 흘렀던가는 알려고 하지 말기 바란다. "갈 데가 없어서가 아니라 아침 햇살이 너무 눈에 시리더구나"라며 말끝을 잇지 못하는 어머니 마음을 모두 다 헤아릴 수는 없을 터이니.

There were admittedly some initial concerns whether illustrator Choi Jae-eun, born and raised in an urban environment, and educated in New York City, would be able to properly capture the story's setting, placed in the early 1960s in a very remote, mountainous region in the Korean countryside. Nevertheless, Choi's excellent illustration abilities were considered absolutely necessary to recreate the Namdo through realistic expression without artifice and to convey the true nature of Korean motherhood, which forms a major subplot of this work.

The straightforward composition and color scheme Choi used in her illustrations can be seen as a strategic decision of hers to enhance the image of a mother who looks pitiful to the point of being an embarrassment. It also expresses the many sentiments surrounding the maternal figure in the Namdo region, where people find it impossible to directly criticize or wholly accept this ragged afterimage of a mother from such a time period.

There is, however, much more to Choi's pictures than these disjointed images. In the section that evokes the "snowy road" in the mother's heart, which uses the dresser mirror as a path to serenely link the past and the present, readers can almost feel the snowflakes slicing through the piercing dawn wind, blowing across the pages. There are such images as the mother's hair neatly raised in a bun as she walks along the snowy morning road with her son; her traditional rubber shoes wrapped in straw in the close-up of her retracing the two sets of footprints in the snow; the soft pink hue of the scarf wrapped around her neck. All of these portrayals, contrasted with the gentle and warm love found in the mother's hands that are as rough as tree bark, possess the power to move readers' hearts.

One shouldn't ask whether tears actually flow down the mother's cheeks as she vainly stares at the desolate, morning sky, since it is impossible to fully understand this mother's heart, whose words drift off softly when she says that it "was the blinding sunlight of morning, not the uncertainty of finding a place to live"

이나미 · 북프로듀서, 크리에이티브 디렉터/스튜디오 바프
Rhee Nami · Book Producer and Creative Director at Studio BAF